DREAMS OF SPEAKING

Gail Jones

Dreams of Speaking

Harvill Secker
LONDON

Published by Harvill Secker, 2006

4 6 8 10 9 7 5 3

© Gail Jones, 2006

First published in Great Britain in 2006 by
HARVILL SECKER
Random House
20 Vauxhall Bridge Road
London SW1V 2SA

Random House Australia (Pty) Limited
20 Alfred Street, Milsons Point, Sydney,
New South Wales 2061, Australia

Random House New Zealand Limited
18 Poland Road, Glenfield,
Auckland 10, New Zealand

Random House South Africa (Pty) Limited
Isle of Houghton, Corner of Boundary Road & Carse O'Gowrie,
Houghton 2198, South Africa

The Random House Group Limited Reg. No. 954009
www.randomhouse.co.uk

A CIP catalogue record for this book is available from the British Library

ISBN 9781843431978 (from Jan 2007)
ISBN 1843431971

Papers used by Random House are natural, recyclable products made from
wood grown in sustainable forests; the manufacturing processes conform
to the environmental regulations of the country of origin

Typeset by Palimpsest Book Production Limited, Polmont, Stirlingshire
Printed and bound in Great Britain by Clays Ltd, St Ives plc

'Let us sculpt in hopeless silence all our dreams of speaking'

Fernando Pessoa, *The Book of Disquiet*

PART ONE

I

It felt like space walking.

It felt like a suspension of the rarest kind, and she saw herself a floaty astronaut, strung in airless dark, supernatural, abstract, buoyed on who-knows-what force to dangle heroically meaningless. There would be a silver visor reflecting everything, and she would be a shape, just a shape, in what had seemed to her always a sorrowful enterprise. Anything in slow motion, she decided, was intrinsically sorrowful. Even as a child she knew this. Even as a child she saw on television how sadly astronauts moved, smitten by world-historical symbolism and the gaze of too many invisible cameras. Their arms were heavy prongs and their heads ridiculous. Their outsized suits were cartoonish and strange. The engineered umbilicus was truly poignant. Yet they moved — she knew it — incomparably. She was seven when she began to see them in daydreams. They belonged to moments of dismay and quiet estrangement. Alone in their silent worlds. Completely alone.

Alice moved to the bedroom window and stood shivering in her pyjamas, watching the 3 a.m. world outside. From her first-floor apartment she surveyed a wedge of the street. It dozed in its own inky pool, awash with blue dark, dissolved into itself. Someone irresponsible had left a sprinkler running. There was a murmurous spray and tiny arcs of light.

The street was empty, the air was brittle and clear. Beyond sight, traffic moved in a black stream along an arterial road. How terrible to live there, Alice thought, where it is never still. To see car after car, to sense the relentlessness of machines. Night-shift workers perhaps, milkmen, the sleepless, the demented.

Alice looked at the sky and sniffed at the heavens. Night seemed to swallow her. It was true, then, her ancient, girlish understanding. Grief is like space walking. It is nothing terrestrial. Laws of gravity alter, and bodies tilt and float away.

*

She had grown up in a city full of light.

It was not a city anyone cared for – not even a city by most estimations – but it lay on the edge of Western Australia, complacent in its remoteness, implacably there, an entire desert between it and the distant cities of the east. On promotional films it was composed of aerial shots, which showed at their centre a vast shining river, nowadays full of yacht sails and windsurfers and ferries bearing tourists. On sunlit days the river refracted light everywhere: there was never a city so bleached into a mirage of itself. Alice loved the river and its special effects. All that was solid melting into air. The material assertion – built on mining money and pastoral seizure and colonialist pride – dispersed into bone-tinted visions and a paradoxical sense of deathless impermanency. Tycoons made their homes here, and migrants from Britain and South Africa. It was a refuge for white people who wished not to remember. It was safe, everyone said. It was a good place to raise children.

The city at the edge of the desert had no monuments or community. It was pragmatic, secular, dun-coloured, dull. So for Alice the river had been a spiritual compensation. She

4

cycled its edges, swam its jellyfish pools, she sat still, looking into its luminous distances, and found in the rippling dissolution a space of repose. When she was a teenager she learned at last to windsurf, and joined others who sped across the water in a flash of spray, bisecting small waves with decisive strokes. Catching the fickle wind, leaning her body into acrobatic balance, finding the velocity of so simple and swift a craft, made Alice feel euphoric. Sometimes she laughed as she rode the water. Sometimes the wind off the river was so strong and the air so alive she felt she was surfing into something elemental.

As an adult she rented an apartment by the river. It was not within view, but she knew it was there. A mere five-minute walk took her to its shore. At night, when she could not sleep, she was comforted by knowing that the water flowed nearby, dark with an oily blackness, silent, deep, dragging with river-tenderness a world of lost things, the silt of history and the plastic detritus of the present, night yearnings, dreams, drowned and buoyant possibilities, misty shapes that would resolve only in some future lens.

*

What was it Mr Sakamoto had said that day?
Everyone needs inside them an ocean or a river.

*

Just before sunrise there was an explosion of birdsong. Wattle-eaters and magpies claimed the world. Alice could hear them call diagonally across the sky, their sounds a crisscrossing net that fell over the morning. She had made herself a coffee and was sitting like a child, knees drawn up protectively against her chest, staring at nothing in particular. She watched her book-filled room gather yellowish light. The spines of the books were a kind of reproach – a life lived too inwardly, too much alone, too given over to perplexity and complication.

Must ring Norah, Alice thought.

On the table, against the wall, lay the pages of her manu-script, a book almost completed. She had written it in feverish excitement, contracted into purpose, fierce, engaged, absorbing the whole world, and now it seemed to her like so much litter, like something dead and unconnected. Perhaps all authors come to despise the words they trail behind them. Or perhaps this feeling was another consequence of her astronautical detachment. She wanted latency, silence. The stacked pages of the manuscript glowed faintly in the dawn. She must send them, or dispose of them. Those pages, her words.

When she had finished her coffee Alice threw her cup towards the sink and heard it smash noisily against the wall. An act of casual destruction, which she will now have to clear away. Refusing to consider the mess, Alice pulled on jeans and a T-shirt, padded down the stairs, and left the apartment build-ing, neat as a thief.

Already the paths along the river were full of cyclists and joggers, heading with moral earnestness into the new day. The joggers looked grim and determined, as joggers invariably do; the cyclists were humped in speedy condescension. Alice turned west, with the sun behind her and a salty breeze from the Indian Ocean detectable in the air. Before her the river was flush with gold; it swelled like a live thing against the stone embankment. People moving in the distance wore a pelt of shine. The trees were aflame, the sky was stretched like cellophane. Yet none of this — how keenly Alice felt it — seemed to her beautiful. Even when dolphins appeared in the little bay, a family of four, curving in and out of the water with the fluent solemnity she had always admired, Alice was unmoved. A jogger, a young man, brushed her shoulder accidentally as he pounded past. In his streaming wake floated song lines from his over-loud headphones. Something about becoming nothing. Something about wanting to be woken. She recognised the song: 'Wake Me Up Inside'.

Alice turned back into the light wishing it would scorch her.

★

'It doesn't matter anyway,' Norah declared.

Alice had been trying to persuade her sister to exchange names.

'But it does matter. It does.'

In her seventh year, the year, she understood later, of one's most radical perceptions, Alice realised that Norah was surely her own true name, and that her sister was an Alice. She deplored the fact that her name had a storybook precedent, that it sounded hard and fragile, like cold glass cracking, that it was girlish, with frills and an upstanding bow. Norah sounded like wind, like the breath of a mystery.

But her sister was stubborn and would not be persuaded. Alice pinched her, and knocked her down, and when the younger girl began to sob, stooped to comfort her, asserting her power once again.

With her wrong name she grew, as misnamed children will. Alice was the clever one, declared her parents; Norah was arty. The sisters competed in everything and were not companionable. In their humble iron and weatherboard house in the suburbs, they quarrelled and fought. Pat and Fred Black, their nice-enough parents, wondered what they had done wrong to produce such warring creatures, who scratched at each other's faces and destroyed each other's possessions. But in the adolescent years, when they gloomily expected an intensification of hostilities, the girls one day – miraculously – became firm friends. Alice and Norah looked into each other's faces, and found there no mirror, but a reassuring encounter. Their violent language

7

fell away; their animosity, sharp as acid, diluted and evaporated. It was one of those homecomings, like falling in love. It was a confirmation of the intimacies held within separate beings, waiting to be disinterred, waiting only to be recognised. The sisters began dressing alike and walked with linked arms. They kissed in the street, swapped notes and confidences. And when, at fifteen, Alice tried again to exchange names, Norah's adamant refusal won her respect. Under a high pergola of blooming wisteria — their father's pride and joy — they embraced and laughed.

'So I'm stuck with it,' said Alice. 'No chance of a bribe?'

Norah hauled herself up, stood erect on the outdoor table, and announced in a loud voice: 'I am Norah! For ever!'

Alice knew she would carry for the rest of her life this moment of reconciliation, this image of her sister's broad face, haloed by a ceiling of mauve flowers, defiant in the act of possessing her own name.

Norah almost fell when she descended too quickly. Alice caught her, toppling, and they were both bruised against their parents' ugly hard furniture. In the smattered space of blown petals they groaned, and then they laughed.

*

As she was clearing the mess of smashed cup, Alice cut her hand. She gashed her palm when kneeling, she steadied herself, and leaned directly onto a shard.

'Fuck.'

The word, Mr Sakamoto said, to be reserved only for unanticipated annoyances.

Alice pressed the wound closed, but blood dripped onto the floor, amazingly bright. She became efficient in this ordinary crisis, scooping the fragments of shattered cup, wiping away the blood, binding her hand — the right — with a nearby teatowel. Exhaustion swept over her. This was all too difficult. Even her own small world had begun offering wounds.

It was full light now, and morning, but Alice decided to return to sleep. Nursing her wrapped hand, she lay back on the couch and closed her eyes, falling immediately into a dream: something lurid, tormenting, which she will later forget. When she woke, an hour later, aroused by throbbing and blood from her hand soaking into her pants at the crotch, she was overcome irrelevantly by the recollection of a childhood event.

She was ten years old and had been travelling with her family in the country, heading for the south coast. She and Norah were squabbling in the back of the car; their exasperated parents kept turning their heads to scold. They were driving through karri forest and Alice remembered the straight high trees, the shafts of filtered blue light, the sense of magical transportation as shadows and brightness flitted by. She had leaned her cheek against the icy clear glass of the window and thought how wonderful it was that someone had invented cars, how wonderful to slide like this, past whole forests, through tunnels of trees. But then her father braked suddenly, they were all flung forward, and in the same instant she heard an abrupt and hollow-sounding collision. The car had hit a kangaroo, which had bounded across its path. Fred pulled to the side of the road, his hands trembling on the steering wheel, his face ashen with shock. He wound down the window and looked back to see what he had done. The kangaroo was large and grey, fallen onto its shank, unable to move. It looked intact and unharmed, but blood was seeping in a shiny pool from somewhere beneath it. The head was cocked. The eyes were glazed and accusatory.

'Do something,' said Pat. Her voice was nervous, taut.

It was remarkable, Alice thought afterwards, how there are actors and watchers.

Fred and Alice together left the car and walked back up the road to inspect the kangaroo. As it saw them approach, it became helplessly agitated; its paws began to shake and it kicked with one leg. Alice saw that her father was close to tears, but she felt she must, since she was the clever one, act in a sensible way.

'We have to do it, Dad. We have to put it out of its misery.'

These words had arrived with glossy facility from television or cinema. Alice was surprised at how easily she knew what to say, and how simple it was to announce an execution. She will wonder, later on, what channels open in mouths that speed into everyday life these lines of screen-written dialogue. Her own voice sounded synthesised, produced by a machine. Power sounded like this. Decisiveness. Authority.

Fred and Alice decided they would hit the kangaroo's head with the back of a small axe they carried in the car. When they returned to the car, Pat and Norah had both begun to cry.

'We have to do it,' Alice repeated. 'We have to put it out of its misery.'

Her father leaned into the boot, and retrieved the axe. He stood poised for a moment, and looked like a storybook wood-chopper, but for his white and stricken face and his unsteady hands. He would never act, she knew. Without speaking Alice took the axe from her father. She strode off, up the road, intent on action. She was animated, purposeful. Behind her the car was ticking as it cooled. A sour smell of burned rubber lingered on the road.

The grey kangaroo kicked again in a vain effort to escape, surprisingly lively, given its loss of blood. Fred dragged it by the tail onto the grassy verge, leaving on the bitumen a slick smear of red. Alice considered its silence. Perhaps these animals were mute. Perhaps its injuries had sealed it prematurely in a deathly quiet. She realised she was grateful it had not cried out, or whimpered, or made some endearing pet-like sound. Alice did not look at the face. She brought the blunt end of the axe down upon its head, once, twice, and then a third time, before the skull smashed and the animal at last quivered, and was still. The face lay to one side, averted, as if in private sorrow. Alice felt the sweat on her hands, knew her own tough heartbeat, heard the amplified hush that was death, ringing through the forest.

Her father stood beside her, softly weeping. He looked mottled and old, and had a tremulous, vulnerable aspect. He took the axe from Alice's hands, wiped it on the grass, first this side, then that, with what seemed to her an unfeasibly slow motion, and then they walked side by side, back to the car, saying not a word. Alice's mother and sister were wiping their tears, each with a fist of crumpled tissues. There was such distress in that small, metallic space. The way cars heat up with emotion, their mysterious responsiveness.

As Alice slid into her seat, Norah hissed, 'Murderer!' Alice fell back into herself, wondering whether life was always going to be like this, full of sudden and irreversible things, full of an anguish contained in the small events within families, in bloody accidents, in difficult moments, that force one member of the family to act, and then to feel ashamed. And not just momentarily, but for ever and ever.

*

Alice's hand was being stitched by a competent doctor. She had been embarrassed to admit that it was a domestic mishap.

'Quite a gash,' said the doctor in an admiring tone, pleased no doubt to be relieved of flu cases and colicky infants, faced instead with a serious rupture of flesh.

Her palm was cross-stitched in a way that recalled B-movies.

'A monster,' she said.

'Pardon?' the doctor asked, not wanting a reply.

He bound the wound with white gauze and gave his handiwork a pat.

'There,' he said conclusively.

Alice tucked her hand under her armpit, as children used to do after a caning. She walked outside into the summery air, looked up at the cloudless sky, saw an aeroplane climb across the blue in a high lyrical curve, and remembered once again that she must ring Norah.

*

They had loved each other, and then diverged, dragging their lives behind them in entirely separate directions. Norah went to art school and met there a student architect, Michael, by whom she became pregnant within four months of their meeting. They moved in together and their child, David, was born much too early. In those precarious first months, Michael and Norah transformed into a haggard, obsessive couple, strained with new love, tired beyond measure, desperately preoccupied with their ailing baby. Alice had visited them often, but felt excluded. Michael looked at her suspiciously; Norah struggled to make conversation. When Alice held her nephew she felt a momentary pang of terror: the fragility of the infant – which seemed to her crimson, insensate and perpetually wailing – was awful to contemplate. She realised maternal tenderness was an overweening obligation, some contract that, having been entered into, could not be broken. Norah had twin violet rings beneath her eyes and had never before seemed so unhappy. Michael had begun smoking, much to Norah's disgust, and blew furious threads of foul air about the house in a wretched rebellion against his own feelings of entrapment.

When a year later a second child, Helen, arrived, Alice worried that her sister might capsize entirely, and become so removed from her, so indentured to baby-land, and Michael, and the vague abductions of self that seemed part of early maternity, that they would be permanently and irretrievably estranged. But this time it was different. Helen was a fat, happy baby, bent on conjuring harmony. She slept, she sucked and, at the right moment, she smiled. Norah grew confident and enjoyed her mothering, recovering the backchat to her sister's teasing, dispensing wit and intelligence, seizing for herself small acts of emancipation. The difference too was in Alice's presence at the birth. Because Michael had been ill with pneumonia, Norah called on Alice to attend, and she had performed not so much the role of support, as that of witness. For most of the labour, Norah seemed barely aware of her presence, massively sealed in her own irresistible upheaval, and Alice had simply squeezed her hand and supplied encouraging platitudes. Nothing prepared Alice for her niece's advent. She came as from a mouth, like a kind of fleshly word. There was Norah's stiff agony, the red lips releasing, and then this completed and precious new being. She was lustrous with fluid and shiny with life. Norah lifted herself on her elbow and was caught in the rapture of the moment. The sisters clasped each other and were unceremoniously elated.

So this would be their pattern. They would zigzag in and out of closeness and distance, retreating, converging, retreating and converging. For every faraway time, or loss, there would be a return, there would be propinquity.

When the placenta arrived, Alice was shocked to see this meaty remnant of life, delivered in a second birthing, in hideous imitation. Somehow she had not imagined this stage beforehand. Norah seemed not to notice. She held her daughter, wrapped like a pupa, close to her face. When Alice turned to look, they were a world of just two.

★

Cycling was difficult, against the wind, now that Alice could not use her right hand. She rode slightly upright, tensely pedalling. It was a fine, light morning, which would later subside into a dense narcotic heat. As she turned the corner, swinging in a semicircle, she saw that Norah was in the garden, waiting for her arrival. She wore loose Indian pants and a funky shirt Alice had not seen before. They waved simultaneously, Alice sending up her wounded hand like a flag of surrender. Norah's hair, she noticed, showed no signs of growing back; she still looked newly vulnerable and pitifully thin. Something in the appearance of her skull's definite shape filled Alice with tenderness. The blank bone of her sister's cranium. This obscene exposure.

The children were at kindergarten, and Norah was in high spirits.

'What's this?' she asked, pointing to the bandage.

'Stupid,' Alice replied. 'A stupid accident.'

'I should be so lucky,' Norah said, and kissed her sister on both cheeks, in the French manner they enjoyed, and turned to lead her inside.

Now that her chemotherapy was ended, Norah seemed sprightly, rejuvenated, like a prisoner on reprieve. She set before Alice a pot of tea and a plate of scones.

'Quite the little housewife.'

'No way. I've started painting again. I'll show you later.'

Alice was abashed by Norah's easy affirmation.

'I still can't believe it,' she said. 'I still can't believe that no

14

one told me you were ill. I would have returned. I would have come back immediately. Why didn't Michael ring? Or Mum, or Dad?'

'I've told you already. Drop it, Alice. Besides, telephones are such mendacious things . . .'

Norah was slicing the scones in two, coating each half extravagantly with strawberry jam and cream. 'You only live once,' she said lightly. Her appetite had returned.

'My doctor says,' she added more gravely, 'that you should get checked. It's unusual, so young, and after two babies. It runs in families, apparently. Sisters and mothers, he said. I'll make an appointment at the clinic. We'll go together.'

They consumed the scones messily, like schoolgirls, like their naughty past selves. The tea was sweet and comforting. Norah chatted about her children. David could now count, Helen was an artist, like her mother. There were daubed livid images and colourful tantrums.

After a lapse in conversation Alice found herself asking: 'Do you remember, when we were small, that time our car hit a kangaroo?'

There was a pause between them. Norah took a sip of tea and raised her blue skull. 'Of course,' she said. 'You were brutal. I hated you.'

'I was only . . .' Alice hesitated, 'putting it out of its misery.' She heard her old words recur, like an emphatic exculpation.

'Perhaps,' Norah conceded. 'I looked out through the back window and saw your arm rise, and rise again. Dad just stood there. Your energy at killing frightened me. I saw the streak of blood on the road and was sick at the sight of it. When you returned to the car you seemed so changed.'

'I'm sorry,' Alice said pointlessly.

She did not know what she was apologising for. She sat before her sister, her sister who was bald with her own suffering and entirely without self-pity, who bore the indefensible treachery of her own body with poise and good humour, who baked scones, who was generous and adored her children, feeling like a culprit of some sort. Feeling guilty. So much lay between siblings, so much obstinate history. So much overlapped in inexpressible ways.

Norah leaned forward. 'So when are you going to tell me about Mr Sakamoto?'

*

The Invention of cellophane

A Monsieur Jacques E. Brandenberger, a Swiss man with a hefty nose, a large moustache and an imperious mien, was one day seated in a restaurant when a customer at the next table spilled wine on the tablecloth. Being both a textile engineer and a man of daring ingenuity, he conceived at that moment the invention of a flexible, transparent and waterproof material, which might protect tablecloths ever after from the clumsiness of diners. He began by applying liquid viscose to cloth, but found it too stiff and impractical a solution. By 1908, however, he had invented a machine for making transparent sheets and cellophane was born! The same Jacques E. Brandenberger, who had witnessed the inspirational spilling of wine, developed a flexible film and two years later had also invented the visor component of gas masks that, in the largesse of war, bought him his ultimate fortune.

This was in one of the first e-mails Mr Sakamoto sent. His style was florid and archaic, his disposition melodramatic. His written English was accomplished, a tribute, he once claimed, to the private tutor his father indulgently hired – a man from Manchester, a Mr O'Toole, who arrived in Japan with frayed cuffs and a class-traitorish regard for high-flown expressions and old-fashioned syntax.

'Another time,' Alice said to Norah. 'I'll tell you another time. Would you like to know, instead, about Alexander Graham Bell, inventor of the telephone?'

*

The white heat blasted her as she rode. She moved her body steadily, driving herself into the glare. Norah had been fulsome, open, and Alice had been secretive. She was not intentionally so; there was a kind of block to her feelings, an abysmal suppression, and a superstition, perhaps, that she should not recover this man too soon by formulations of words. Against the waste of death, no language availed. No words, easy as breath, routinely available, slipped forth to settle her insurgent feelings. She must wait. She must know. She must know exactly what to say.

Alice bent her head like a penitent beneath the assaulting sun. Her legs were robotic. She barely looked where she was going.

2

One year ago, without knowing it, she had been travelling to meet him. Alice was flying to Europe, following darkness around the planet in her north-westerly projection. She would have a doubled night – the nothing-space of jet flight was freighted with black magic, so that passengers bore stoically their extended nocturne, relinquishing the ordinariness of time, relinquishing good meals and intelligent conversation, for this wearisome, dull, zombie imprisoning. The habit of detachment was useful in such situations. In the incessant roar of the wind tunnel of flight, Alice watched the serried strangers around her. They were fixed in crepuscular gloom onto screens or magazines, each locked away, looking sad, in a solipsistic reverie. Alice wondered what form of modernity this might be, and how she might include it in her book. Her project was presumptuously entitled *The Poetics of Modernity* and she wished to study the unremarked beauty of modern things, of telephones, aeroplanes, computer screens and electric lights, of television, cars and underground transportation. There had to be in the world of mechanical efficiency some mystery of transaction, the summoning of remote meanings, an extra dimension – supernatural, sure. There had to be a lost sublimity, of something once strange, now familiar, tame.

The lights switched off and passengers seemed instantly to sleep. They had become sluggish, bored. Now they met the extra night with their eyes closed, their heads thrown back, their mouths slackly agape like codfish. Alice watched movies of diverting inanity. The little screen before her was a hideaway to hunker into. At some point she rose to stretch her legs and found the whole population asleep. She crept gingerly up the aisle and saw — as in a science-fiction movie in black and white — that in their steel and aluminium tube everyone was insensible. It was as if the plane was governed by alien air or some creaturely intention. A posthumous blue washed over bodies, faces. Hoping for a coffee, Alice made her way to the hostesses' enclave, and discovered two uniformed women also fast asleep, one of them with her cheek propped against the shoulder of the other. She retreated quietly, wondering about the automation of planes, how they stayed up, anyway, what antigravitational devices kept them here, defying all instinct, hurtling like a thrown thing through distorted ever-darkness.

About 4 a.m. in no-time the lights came on. Groggy passengers roused to a putative breakfast. Before the trays with their standard selections and plastic implements were swept away, Alice hailed a hostess and requested a view of the cockpit. She showed her university card, and announced dishonestly that she was writing a book about flight. It was almost true, she reasoned. Almost plausible. The hostess, who was bottle-blonde, in her forties and weary with life, eyed Alice suspiciously and said she would see. Within ten minutes, however, Alice was being led to the front of the plane, past the first-class passengers in their absurdly wide seats, through dark-green curtains and a digitally coded door and on into the cockpit. There she met the two pilots, Walter and Briggs. Before her, in a cramped dome of lights, like the church of some peculiar, unorthodox religion, Alice saw a curve of endless black sky, and far below, a carpet of uneven lights, profuse and lovely. Bright forms constellated and slid beneath them. Patterns of flash, ardent glows, electrified destinations.

'Frankfurt,' Briggs announced, matter-of-factly.

Alice felt her old-fashioned heart was racing. Here, in this bubble of impossibility, suspended in heaven, she saw with inhuman gaze how marvellous was this invention, how bold its assertion into pure space. She sensed propulsion and the churning of gigantic engines. She sensed circuits, sparks, powerful calculations. She felt irresponsible delight in her view of Frankfurt. All around her, intricate dials and buttons dramatised the algebra of flight.

'I feel like God,' she said quietly. This, from an atheist.

Walter and Briggs simultaneously swivelled their heads to see her. There was a still, awkward moment, then Captain Walter laughed.

'Me too,' he confessed. His face was ruddy in the glow of the cockpit lights. He smiled wry approval. Captain Briggs blew into his palms: a Muslim at prayer.

The pilots asked Alice if she had any questions, practical or theoretical, but she could think of none. Her pretext was at risk. But neither seemed to doubt the legitimacy of her invasion. She simply stood behind them, importunate, imposturing, watching the night illimitably unfold. She was watching speed, watching modernity.

*

There is little as artificially brilliant as a neon sign.

Pause and consider. The glow is incomparable. *Motel* has never before seemed so numinous. *Drinks. Dancing Girls. All-Nite Bar.* When they were first shown in America, people stopped in the street and stared. 'Liquid fire,' they whispered. 'Liquid fire.' Since the seventeenth century scientists have observed that certain gasses could be caused, through motion or voltage, to emit a pale glow, a magical quiver. But it was a French man, Georges Claude, who first applied an electrical charge to a sealed tube of neon gas, to create an entirely new-fangled lamp. He saw before him luminosity at the level of atoms, each agitated in a new, utterly sparkly, life. Neon is rather a rare gaseous element – in the air we breathe it is but one part in 65,000. Yet separated, it has this illuminate capacity: even in atmospheric conditions it glimmers bright red. Georges Claude first displayed his invention to the public in Paris, in wintry December 1910. Crowds cheered and clapped. *Sacré Bleu!* they chorused. They were applauding the very transformation of air. Their eyes were lit with novel amazement. City streets would never be the same again. Pinks rosier, intensified. Blues from outerspace. Words written above buildings in purest white light. On or about December 1910, everything changed.

*

Mr Sakamoto had raised his glass of red wine.

'The difficulty with celebrating modernity,' he declared, 'is that we live with so many persistently unmodern things. Dreams, love, babies, illness. Memory. Death. And all the natural things. Leaves, birds, ocean, animals. Think of your Australian kangaroo,' he added. 'The kangaroo is truly unmodern.'

Here he paused and smiled, as if telling himself a joke.

'And sky. Think of sky. There is nothing modern about the sky.'

*

21

Sliding down from the black sky, Alice arrived at Charles de Gaulle Airport, racked with sleeplessness. In the passport line she saw that others, too, were bleary, and talked in the thick, muffled tones of the half-awake. Stephen would be waiting beyond the lines, watching for her arrival. She had asked him not to come, but knew he would be there, expecting to touch her, anxious for a kiss. The line moved slowly. When at last she was through, she remembered her luggage, and stood, waiting once more, at the carousel. A kind of desolation suddenly overtook her. What would she say to Stephen? How would she tell him? When her case circled before her she didn't recognise it at first, then chased, lurching. The conveyer belt rumbled on with its parcels of lives, tagged and ribboned.

Airports divide people into the leaving and the arriving. The leaving were jittery, bought drinks and unnecessary duty-free items and moved in an intermediate consciousness, halfway gone. The arriving, dulled by their own motionless speeding, relieved to be on the earth and clutching their legitimating documents, were compliant and subdued. In a casual fumble Alice dropped her passport on the floor. She looked down and saw it — a royal-blue square with the kangaroo and emu standing posed in the centre. It was like a surrealist object, displayed in its oddity and drastically misplaced.

Stephen waited at the barrier with a bouquet of flame-coloured tulips. He hailed Alice at once, and pushed his way forward. There was a moment when they were estimating each other's appearance. He looked handsome — she could not deny it — in his long winter coat and scarf; and was no doubt noticing that Alice carried in her face the raddled emotions of swooping around the globe. Imperative loud-speaker announcements smothered their hallos.

'You look great,' Alice heard.

Stephen leaned to her left side and kissed her cautiously.

'You too.'

They caught the shuttlebus to the railway station, juddering all the way, jolted at each stop, and then Stephen produced two tickets and carried her case through to the platform. Dawn was breaking as the train rolled towards the city. Stephen reached for Alice's hand and she tried her best to attend to his friendly chat. He spoke of mutual friends, a new jazz club he had discovered, an article he had published. Alice watched a young black man with dreadlocks bob to his own music, held hidden in his pocket and streaming to him privately through thin yellow wires. He looked possessed, mystical. Music. Why was it she still knew nothing about music? Outside, in a fleeting view, she saw a gypsy encampment in old railway carriages, a mother washing her child with water from a metal bucket, a man in a dirty coat gesticulating insanely at the sunrise.

A neon sign flashed by: an advertising epiphany. Alice was waiting for Stephen to ask her about the flight, so that she could say: *I was in the cockpit. It was like a church. I saw the city of Frankfurt appear gorgeously, as a figment of light.*

But he did not ask, and instead filled the uncertain space between them with his own preoccupations and talkative nervousness. When they drew near Châtelet, in the city centre, Stephen simply said: 'Come to my place. Stay with me.'

Alice replied that she was meeting the woman who had the key to her studio apartment. She would see him later, she promised. Later. After she had slept.

They parted at the Métro. Alice watched Stephen diminish, looking forlorn, as her train sped off in the direction of St-Paul. Blur enveloped the crowd on the platform. The booming tunnel sucked the train into darkness. In Alice's hands the bunch of tulips was damaged, frayed at the edges.

*

Let me tell you, *wrote Mr Sakamoto*, about Chester F. Carlson.

He was a man passionately at odds with the world's brute singularity. He wanted the duplication or multiplication of all things. In part this was a peculiar, personal response to his increasing baldness, which tormented him with its prematurity and depreciation of his appearance. Daily he rubbed his palm over his vulnerable head, and daily felt the boundaries of his body were becoming mangy, unsure. He combed his hair in ingenious ways, but nothing disguised the radiant absence. In the end, he took to wearing expensive tweed caps, which he decided were a flattering and acceptable substitution for hair.

A law student, he lived with his widowed mother and four marmalade cats, all pleasingly alike. In his spare time Chester dabbled in chess and invention, and in 1937 developed a copying process, feline inspired, based on electrostatic energy. Words reproduced on a page in just a few minutes in a process he called xerography, from the Greek for 'dry writing'. But no one was interested and no one invested. IBM and the US Signal Corps turned him down. After eight long years, by which time he had no hair left at all, an investor at last signed up, calling itself the Xerox Corporation.

In due course, Chester F. Carlson was so wealthy that his baldness was inconsequential. He tugged at his lapels and addressed the press: 'When I filed the patent application,' he declared, 'I knew I had a very

big tiger by the tail.' His eyes glistened with moisture as he thought of the lookalike cats, beloved repetitions, to which his changed circumstances and wealth had made no difference at all. They loved him just the same. They loved his singularity.

*

She had met Stephen at university, when they were both in their second year of study. He had long hair, which fell diagonally across his face, and an inward, secluded attitude that challenged women to break through. Unaware of his attractiveness, he was doubly desirable. When they first spoke she detected in his voice a gravelly tone, a kind of old-man timbre inconsistent with his youth. He was studying philosophy – which somehow fitted his incommensurate voice. She was studying literature.

They fell into bed together almost immediately, with a sense of enormous relief and easy companionship. Sexual relationships at university have an unprecedented and never-to-be-recovered-again liberty, unencumbered, mutually explorative, ideologically confirmed. In the energy of their congress, they thought themselves heroic. Afterwards, they would lie sideways on the bed, their heads tilted backwards, smoking joints, exchanging facile aphorisms about the meaning of life, kissing and giggling and wasting time. It was always afternoon. There were always specks and particles in the air, imperishable, resonant, blazing up with the unseen vitality they now detected in every thing.

Alice remembers this: once, after they had made love, Stephen began suddenly to weep. She stroked his cheek and murmured consolation, but her lover remained obdurately unconsoled. He had been in love, at fourteen, with a girl who was hit by a car. She was only twelve. They said she had died instantly. In his home town on the south coast, in a former whaling community, this girl had become an emblem of loss. Everyone remembered her. Everyone mourned. She became more cherished, he said, as the years went by. She became their symbol. There was a park named after her, a park of straggly pink rosebushes, blown to smithereens by the fierce sea wind.

Alice lay back, looking at the ceiling. She was learning that every life has its secret collisions, that in even the most self-possessed of men, there are also these vacancies and lamentations. Alice rolled onto Stephen's body, stretching out to encompass him, so that their limbs matched part to part, like a photocopy. She kissed his tearful eyes, and knew for the first time that in every intimacy there are these spirit presences, which rise up, revenant, even in lovemaking. She had wanted to say to Stephen that she understood his grief, but in those days she did not.

'What was her name?' she asked. 'This twelve-year-old girl.'

'Her name was Alice,' said Stephen, in a low rough voice.

*

When she arrived at the studio Alice found that it was no more than an ascetic box. There was a single bed, a table and two upright chairs; there was a modest kitchen to one side, in which nestled a toy-sized refrigerator and a small gas burner with two rings. She tapped the red gas bottle, which resembled an aqualung, and realised that she had no idea how to gauge its fullness. From the first floor, the studio faced onto a narrow street, and from the window Alice could see a secondary school, disgorging its pupils for a noisy break. They hung around flirting and smoking; their voices rose in dispersing syllables.

This is perfect, Alice thought, perfect for writing.

She liked the sense of a clarified existence, in which few possessions, few objects, claimed narrative attention. The air was cold.
Everything was still. In a cupboard Alice found coffee, long-life
milk and a bag of sugar. She brewed coffee over the gas in a
battered saucepan. Her body was strung out, in another time
zone, still operating in the reverse logic of a cross-planetary
biology, but she felt alert, excited. Travel, rush through space,
was her self-enchantment. Relocation into new co-ordinates.
Forfeited certainties. The erotics of strangeness. She couldn't bear
the persistence of the known into stale habituation. Alice sat in
semi-darkness, sipping from her cup.

A few streets away drifted the venerable, khaki-coloured
Seine, older than Europe.

There was no telephone, no television, no labour-saving
appliance. This was where she would imagine, with the
exactitude of deprivation, all those glistening tokens of
modernity, those industrial culminations, that called out to
be described, that were so omnipresent as to have lost their
aura, and their originary dynamic and aesthetic charge. She
made a list of categories:

electrics, mechanics, communication, transportation

Then:

spiritualisation, secularisation, sexualisation

And:

gigantism, miniaturisation, division, replication

vision, sensation, cognition, precognition

tragic, comic, nostalgic, melodramatic

With this slightest of codes, arbitrarily jotted, Alice would
begin to elaborate her poetics of modernity. Sometimes she
would research at the Bibliothèque Nationale; sometimes she
would write as poets do, with the spontaneous embrace of
a seductive metaphor, with the grace and intuition of

selected images, with chance, with blind luck, with errancy and confidence.

Outside there was a sudden crackle of adolescent laughter. It hung in the freezing air, sharp and lucent as icicles.

*

Television is, after all, a box of wonders.

Into its limited cube fly unlimited images; into its receptive channels, with incredible celerity, rush crazy narratives, world events, men and women of unnaturally glossy good looks, historical re-enactments, capitalist extravaganzas, politicians, and singers, and sports heroes by the dozen. In flashy mode it links the grotesque and the mosaic, a combination that allows for hyperbole in all things and the endless, restless fracturing of vision. Viewers, of whom there are billions, are inspired to fanatical devotion or delicious lassitude. The crystal eye finds every sight and pretends to tell every story. There was never a medium so omniscient in its sheer ambition.

The hand-held 'remote' is aptly named. One does not need to touch the television to make it work. From the bed, from the sofa, it is called into action: switching channels is a consequence of the merest pressure, and what opens are sequences, territories, styles, talking heads. Zapped into visibility, for just an instant, every image looks more or less insane. Commercials, especially, carry a lunatic fringe, an appeal to the unhinged you that would dramatise pasta or shampoo, the you that wants to parachute from an aeroplane, or fears the germs in the laundry, or fantasises about solitary travel in protuberant, sexual cars. Humankind cannot bear too much remote incomprehension.

By the light of the television – a spooky indigo glow – one can see mortality itself dance on the faces of entire families.

28

They look arrested, dumb. Death is already claiming them. Flicker is the mode of televisual morbidity.

*

In the middle of the night Alice heard the river for the first time. It met her with a rhythmic, thunderous sound, the sound of volumes of water hurling forward in a muscular curl. When Alice stirred a little, sitting up in the lonely darkness, she realised that the sound was in fact of traffic: a two-way vibrating hum, relentless and inorganic as a Xerox machine. Perhaps it was the *idea* of the river that seemed somehow audible. The distant mystery of nature, persisting in spite of everything. Energies beyond machines. Beyond petrochemical drive.

*

In a toy shop on the Île, Alice found wooden objects of touching simplicity to send to her niece and nephew. They were a pierrot doll with articulated limbs, and a carved oak cat with painted-on eyes. She was not sure which toy she would give to which child. Old-fashioned toyshops aroused in her uncomplicated jubilation. She always entered them, and she always bought something. Behind the counter there was invariably a bespectacled shopkeeper who liked to chat about the virtues of wood. Alice tilted the pierrot at its waist, declaring it lifelike. She thought of her sister, as a six-year-old, bathing a doll. At this moment the past rushed forward like a gust: these anomalous material signs hailed her back, inserted her again into miniature fantasies and the playful animation of wood.

Stephen was early. He sat outside the café in the cold, awaiting her arrival. Alice kissed both cheeks and asked if they could move inside, out of the wind. The glass window of the café returned them as a couple.

'*Anglais?*' asked the waiter, with a perceptible sneer.

'*Australienne,*' Alice replied.

The waiter's attitude changed in an instant. He smiled beneficently. '*Ah! Le kangourou! L'Opéra! L'Aborigène!*'

Stephen looked at the man with withering disparagement, but Alice smiled, and tossed back her head.

'*C'est vrai,*' she said. '*Le kangourou.*'

'Jesus,' Stephen muttered under his breath. 'Do you have to assent and proclaim the stereotype?'

He was ill-tempered. Out of sorts. Alice noticed that he looked as if he hadn't slept.

'It's innocent,' said Alice. 'It's an innocent aesthetic.'

'It's crude. It's a reduction. *L'Aborigène*, what was he thinking?'

They ordered coffee and Stephen subsided into silence. He played with pyramids of sugar; he tore at his paper serviette. Then he barked: 'Why are you here, anyway?' He sounded petulant.

'The work. The grant. They offered me the use of a studio.'

His distress was like clothing: it enveloped him, it altered his shape.

'Can we see each other sometimes?'

'Of course,' said Alice. 'Sometimes.'

'Jesus,' he repeated.

There was nothing Alice could do to alleviate his pain. She would not return to him, even though they were now in the same city, the 'city of romance', the city encrusted — more than the entire continent of Australia — with symbols, clichés.

'Let me show you,' she said, changing the subject, 'what I found in a toyshop. Like objects from the ruins of a lost civilisation.'

She unwrapped the doll and the cat and displayed them on

the table. In the light of the café they had a burnished, pre-historical glow. She touched them carefully, as if they had survived demolition or been retrieved, a humane fragment, from post-war rubble.

'Yes,' said Stephen, relenting. 'Yes, they're charming.'

They ordered second coffees and began to talk more freely. Outside the street was becoming crowded. A tour group flowed by, following a furled umbrella. Each tourist bore a stick-on name tag in the shape of the Eiffel Tower.

Alice and Stephen walked from the café together, passing in front of the Hôtel de Ville. Children were skating on an outdoor ice rink, moving in long, elliptical glides. They inscribed the paths of planets; they constituted a tiny orrery. There was a sparkle to things, an astronomical light. Tourists took photographs with digital cameras and mobile telephones held out before them, like pilgrim offerings.

'I remember', said Stephen, 'sitting on the bank of the river with a book, watching you windsurf. You were unbelievably fast. I looked away for one minute, and you were gone. It was as if you'd been snatched by an invisible force.'

'I was,' said Alice lightly. 'I was snatched by the wind.'

*

The tulips nodded in the jam jar that was their vase.

Strange, how many flowers seemed to have heads. One or two had begun drooping in a melancholy way, bent by time, as people are, and the others stayed upright, uphold-ing their role as sentinels of desire. Alice was pleased to have been given flowers; they were delicately self-sufficient, an edification.

But she dreamed, that second night, that they burst into flames like match-heads, that they materialised as a kind of incendiary device, and began to light first her notebooks and then the table, in a blazing explosion. The fire climbed the curtains of the studio with instant ease and then slid along the floor, liquid as a river. Paint blistered, light bulbs popped, smoke rolled along the ceiling. When the fire at last reached her bed, Alice woke up, her heart banging in her chest. Her skin was aflame in the icy air.

★

The telephone is our rapturous disembodiment. We breathe our selves, like lovers, into its tiny receptacle, and glide out the other end, mere voice, mere function. Wires, currents, satellites, electrical systems: these are the hardware we extend ourselves into, spaced out, underground, alive in the trembling skeins that arch across nations.

Countless conversations are happening at once. Transecting the sky, like lines of flight, like the trajectories of ancient deities borne by eagles or dragons, sentences, words, syllables, sighs – all fly into airy enunciation, becoming messages, becoming text.

The cradle, the handset, the curly extendable wire.

Voices are more lovable on the telephone. Things are said, promises exchanged, that could not bear the weight of incarnation. Voices are also more repulsive, and more distinctly other. One's mother is a monster, one's partner a stranger. Who is to know what impersonations or depersonations are possible? Or what whispered honesties? What mumbled truths?

The dark space of technology between mouths is a space of pure wind; it is a wind that snatches presences, an erosion, a loss.

★

Alice entered the Métro at Concorde and found in the swaying train a ragged musician playing a gypsy violin. He could have been from another century, so metonymic was his face, so Gaulish, so tough. However, he played not the classics, but selections from the Beatles. Uninterested passengers looked away, worried in advance about the moment he would proffer his hat for coins. Then, after the Louvre station, he began playing 'Yesterday'. A thin shabby man stood up from his seat and in European-accented English was all at once singing along. His voice was so authentically plaintive, his manner so piteous, that Alice was overcome by an absurd wish to embrace him and take his head in her lap. The lyrics of 'Yesterday' struck Alice as banal, yet she heard herself humming.

The man was flushed, possibly drunk. He was unsteady on his feet. He rocked with the train, rocked in solitude. Passengers averted their gazes. This man was a violation of good form.

Perhaps it was the mood of the carriage – that shadowy somnolence – perhaps the sombre thin man performing his sadness in humiliation or protest, perhaps simply the adhesive quality of tunes that meet one at moments of vulnerability, all those sticky lyrics that travel around cities, like a web, like a net, like a captivating chain, but Alice found herself humming the song for the next few days.

She had never thought the words amounted to anything more than a tricksy slogan, but now considered, against modernity, the force of *yesterday*, and was stricken with obscure doubt about her project. She pounded the streets, repeating 'Yesterday'.

Mr Sakamoto would later nominate this his favourite Beatles song.

'It combines the simplest of rhymes', he said, 'with the simplest anguish – a man abandoned by his lover – and constructs it all as a spectre of lost time.'

'You're kidding,' Alice had responded.

'Not at all. The idea, think of it, that yesterday might come *suddenly*. Time itself, split open by abandonment.'

Mr Sakamoto had smiled, as he often did upon delivering

his stern pronouncements, so that Alice was unsure whether he was joking or serious.

For now, she was wondering, rather amateurishly, about time and modernity. Wondering how to include it in what she was writing.

And she was haunted by the thin man singing on the train. A man as alone, she could not help thinking, as a drifting astronaut, hauled backwards through space, receding into nothingness, becoming swallowed up, eventually, by airless dark.

*

Stephen appeared at the door. He held a bottle of red wine.

'Have a drink with me,' he pleaded.

So she let him in, and they talked, mostly in blurry reminiscences. When the wine was finished, he leaned over and kissed her, and then again, more fulsomely, so that she responded and clasped him. They undressed with haste, against the cold night air, and fell into each other's bodies as into recovered childhood, unselfconscious, effusive, in the forgetful elation of the moment. Stephen moaned against her neck, full of sadness, full of return. He climaxed with a little cry, Alice, much louder.

When they rolled apart, still breathing with the pace of arousal and activity, Alice said, much too soon: 'This is the last time.'

'I know,' Stephen said. 'You didn't have to say it.'

And then they moved into the easier communion of sleep, deep, companionable, timeless sleep, pressed into each other tightly, on the single bed. At some point Alice awoke, felt Stephen against her body, and heard the micro-sounds that only a lover knows, the quakes of breath and the heaving emissions of dreams, the signals of night-life unfolding and bodily processes. Then she heard through the wall a muffled television in the apartment next door. It sounded like alien communication from Mars. Exclamatory voice fragments, music, percussive notations, all commingled and garbled, unrecognisably weird. These presences swam in the room, insinuated, and stayed all night.

3

The mode of yesterday, *Alice wrote*, is the photographic image. It is always time-bound but out-of-
time, always anachronistic. In its fidelity to moments,
to split-second slices, it carries the gravity of testimony
and the lightness of chance. This paradox endears us:
this is its clever intercession.

The photograph of a child, laughing, pushing her
sister on a swing in a scene of shared play, will carry
for both, into adulthood, the bright trace of their
pasts. They may not remember the moment, but it
will represent them decisively, and they will see
themselves thus. *There was such a moment, such a
scooping of space*, even if now it lies encrypted in all
that has happened since, in all the boisterous life that
rushed afterwards to capture and engulf them.

The photograph of an astronaut pretends to exist in
the future. Initially, its dazzling foreignness, its
supernatural shadows, made the astronaut a figure
beyond time itself. Now we know otherwise. Now this
double-sized man, this cumbrous puppet, is almost
antique. He is so much of his era that, no less than a
uniformed Prussian soldier, or Queen Victoria, or the
hippie Beatles, he is lodged so directly in past time that

no amount of gadgetry unfixes him, or propels him forward.

The photograph of catastrophe halts us. Or it ought to. If there is a necessity to this technology, it is to abet troubled remembering and to drive us to other futures. Shadows infiltrate as surely as light. Do I need to describe these images? They are bleak and indelible. They are detonations. We carry them like tattoos that say 'twentieth century'.

The photograph of someone one loves, as a child: *folded time*. The present is given adorable density; in the face of the beloved rests an earlier face. A boy, leaning cheekily, wearing a beret. Lanky, unpredictable, verging into the tall man who will step forward to embrace you. A girl with freckles and uncontrollable hair. Standing in full sunlight on a white sandy beach, awaiting with eyes open an adult embrace.

*

Stephen once showed Alice a remarkable photograph. It was an image of his father – an official picture of some kind – standing on a whale. When he was a child, he said, his father had worked at the whaling station, slicing into the huge beasts with the blades of giants.

'I hated my father,' said Stephen blankly. 'He was a drunkard, and stank of beer, and would pass out in the kitchen on the linoleum floor. My mother and I would drag him across the diamond shapes – red and black diamonds, I can never forget them – to the living room to heave him onto the sofa. He seemed filthy. Despicable. He dribbled onto his shirt.

'We never got on. My father found my bookishness incomprehensible, but bragged about me to his mates. Egghead, he called me. I was embarrassed, but I was also desperate for his approval. I remember smiling pathetically as I recited the entire periodic table of elements to a group of blokes sitting around in a pub. There was a round of applause, and I bowed, like a concert pianist. My father clapped loudest, and I was proud, and appalled. When he was working at the whaling station, he always stank of blood and raw meat. My mother endured for a while, then suddenly, like that, she just up and left. Just disappeared, leaving me with her sister's address and a brief note of apology. So I was left alone with this dreadful man to whom I had nothing to say. One day, for some reason, I rode my bike out to see him at the whaling station. I had never been there before. The stench hit you from almost a mile away – it was disgusting – viscera, slime, boiled-down flesh. When I approached, I saw the carcass of a whale in mid-slaughter. There were sluice trails for the blood and great saws carving the flesh. Everything looked wet, internal. It seemed to me then the most compelling sight – such a creature, so huge, so complex in its dismemberment. There was a man standing on the very top of the whale, waving. It was my father. I immediately waved back. For some reason I felt a great surge of love. My father, atop a whale. Like a myth. Like a god. After he was killed in the accident one of his workmates gave me this photograph. It brings back that moment. The only moment in my life I can ever remember loving him.'

*

Alice was thinking of Stephen's story as she walked home with her groceries. He had taken to waiting outside her apartment building, seeking to meet her at all times of the day and night. She had imagined their lovemaking was a tender goodbye, but it had unhinged him, somewhat, so that he seemed always to be waiting below the window, without purpose, desultory, standing in the freezing air with his hands in his pockets, shuffling from foot to foot.

'This is harassment,' Alice said, when he pinned her against the wall outside her doorway.

'I just want to talk,' Stephen responded.

'You don't. You want more.'

'Yes, I want more.'

'Leave me alone, Stephen.'

She wondered if she sounded mean. With his face so close, she could tell that he was drinking early in the day. His eyes were red-rimmed. He seemed aged and dishevelled.

'Fuck you.'

'Please,' Alice said quietly. 'I don't want to have to fear you.'

At this, Stephen backed away. He looked down at his feet. His hands were shaking. 'Jesus,' he said.

Alice watched him turn, walk past the school and around the corner. She unlocked her door, then quickly locked it from the inside, her heart pounding as if she had just embraced a lover. Outside an ambulance sped past, pulling its Doppler effect siren behind it. A reminder of how things separated: object and sound.

*

Dear Norah,

There are days here when I truly long for your company. The studio is perfectly adequate, but I find myself alone, talking out loud, and listening to the scraps of late-night television that filter unintelligibly through the ceiling and the walls.

My writing is not going well. I think my project folly and am struck every day by the profundity of orders of experience and sensation that are unconnected to my vainglorious jottings.

39

Stephen is still unaccepting of my distance, and this has led him into misery and me into guilt. It was a mistake, seeing him. Today was only the second day for a long time that he has not stood outside my building – perhaps this is a sign he has given up hope, or come to his senses. I was beginning to dread each time I saw him beneath my window, but now, to be honest, I dread not seeing him, fearing he might have done harm to himself.

Recently I recalled something that I wonder if you too remember. We were quite small – I would have been nine, you would have been seven, and we were on holiday at the beach, in that rugged area near Smith's Point. We must have wandered off together, because we came across a whale skeleton, bleached and partially intact, high up, past the watermark. It was a beautiful thing – sculptural and strange, the ribcage a kind of chamber, the dorsal bones still interlocking with fragments of cartilage, all neatly descending in size, all ivory and unblemished. We stepped inside the belly of the beast, as it were, this blasted, open, monumental space, and were happy together. We were sharing our discovery. Two little girls in floral sundresses and floppy cloth hats. Later we found Dad and with his help laboriously carried one of the backbones up the beach, up through the sand-hills, and back to our hut. I remember it sitting there, outside the hut, with our bathers and goggles, a pure thing, like a stone, a pure deep-water thing. I don't know what became of it. Perhaps we just left it there, where it lay. Do you remember, Norah? Do you know what became of the whale bone?

Do send me news of the children. I have little to

report here – I'm leading a somewhat cloistered life – partly in recoil, I think, from Stephen's behaviour – which has disturbed me more than I care to admit – and partly to find again the quiet sequestration that will enable me to write. And tell me about yourself, and Michael, and how you are both getting on. Your letters are important to me, even though I am a poor correspondent.

My love, as always,
Alice

*

In the middle of the night she heard it again – the sound of the river. Then she listened carefully and once more found that she was mistaken. What she heard this time was the material commotion of the city: sirens, wheels, decelerating buses, footsteps, calls, mobile phones. There was the squeal of an almost-collision and a cry of abuse. There was a plane overhead, dragging decibels in its wake. Vehicles of every kind. The snarl of a motorbike. The rumble of garbage trucks with their brute growling innards, the roll and clack-clack of a late-night skateboard. All this activity in the air, this routine distortion. All this noisy encasement and mobilised intention. Alice wanted silence. She wanted the nullity of deep space. In her bed in Paris, she experienced a twinge of homesickness. Not the longing for a place, so much, as for a space into which her self could be poured, without erasure.

*

'So when did it begin?' Stephen had once asked her. 'This unfeminine interest in machines, in motion, in electrical inventions?'

'There are no beginnings,' Alice said cautiously. 'Only fragments. Only stories.'

She had kissed him at that moment. She needed his questions to prise her, to release her tight secrets. This is the gift of the lover: to permit disclosures.

When she was a very small child, about seven years old, Alice contracted scarlet fever and was confined to the isolation ward of the local hospital. The fear of contagion was not unlike the fear of the devil: imprecise, generalised, bent on marking out the contaminated by macabre tales, tinctures and noxious potions. Or so it seemed, in a simpler version, to a little girl with a pink woollen rabbit and a copy of *Grimm's Fairy Tales*, who was locked in a room with two boys, both likewise infected and untouchable. Ric and James were each two years older than Alice and had already formed a bond of friendship by the time she was admitted. In the daytime they ignored her, at night she heard them whispering in the dark together. But then Ric left, after only a few days, and James was obliged to notice and befriend Alice, if only to alleviate the boredom of their implacably extended days.

The children were allowed no physical contact. Alice's parents and Norah visited, but they stood behind a glass partition, and waved and mouthed messages. Norah held a comic book against the glass, and her mother dangled a brown paper bag of mandarins. James's parents and two brothers also stood in dumb-show, staying only five minutes, clearly unsure how to prolong an expression of love, based on the rigorous spectacle of mime. They too left comic books and a bag of mandarins. James and Alice decided they must have received exact instructions.

For hour on hour it was just the two of them. Since they were forbidden to leave their beds, they at first called to each other across the room, exchanging stories, fears, dreams, intimate confessions. Later they begin to share each other's bed, timing their transgression precisely – just after the morning nurse with the face mask took their temperatures and they knew no one would come for another few hours; and then between their lunch and dinner. They lay close together, talking quietly. Alice read to James from her *Grimm's Fairy Tales*; he shared with her his *How Does it Work?* and *Great Railways of the World*. In their exile the children developed a persuasive, jointly idiosyncratic world, a combination of fabulous transformations, evil characters and life enhanced by modern engineering, by rocket-ships, walkie-talkies, interplanetary transporters. James also had a repertoire of fictitious-sounding sayings – 'Righto! We'll blow them to billyo! Chins up, jolly good chaps!' – which Alice enjoyed but could not understand. Their confabulations were intricate, a mesh of energies, each child competing with the other to add some new embellishment.

Apart from his wondrous books, James also owned a small transistor radio, sheathed in stippled orange plastic. So in between excursions to electrical utopias populated by heroes and villains and princesses disguised as milkmaids, they listened to the Top Forty, and under the blankets, they sang along. When they investigated how the radio worked, it seemed that, like other technologies, it captured the invisible currents of the air. Voices caught roiling sound waves, surfed into the tightly coiled wires of plastic boxes, spun in sparky rings, then emanated gloriously as hits. Origins, properties, functions, destinations: the universe had within it all these regions of vigorous activity, all these gymnastical stretchings and curvings and changings of form. Alice had seen on television how girls no larger than she flew into aerial contortions and abnormal design; it seemed to her impeccable child-logic that there must be ways, or devices, by which all of us might find this hidden motion and elastic space, this land of mutable forces, of turbulent speed, of sheer mechanical wonder.

James was less convinced. 'You need to know things,' he said. 'This is not for everyone. Only *special* people', he explained, 'see the inside of things.'

One day a nurse came by unexpectedly and found James and Alice in bed together. With a violence that was rapid, fierce and entirely instinctual, she seized Alice by the elbow, yanked her from the bed, and with a wide sudden swing slapped the left side of her face. Alice felt a quake within her skull and a hand-sized pain. She fell to the floor, hurt, but was too stunned to cry.

'Don't you ever,' the nurse said tensely, 'don't you *ever* use the same bed again.'

She had grey hair under her cap, fashioned in tight, unnatural curls. She wore an upside-down watch and a badge that said 'BARKER'.

James looked pale with fear. He was stammering an explanation: 'We were only . . .'

But the nurse was not listening. She lifted Alice in a rough bear hug and forcibly dumped her on her own bed.

When Alice developed a swollen black eye and a purple bruise across her cheek, the explanation was that she had awoken at night, was confused, had tangled in her sheets, and fallen from her bed. Norah looked upset behind the glass. Her oval face was on the verge of tearful collapse and Alice saw her touch her own cheek in a kind of signal of compassion. She would tell her, one day, about BARKER, about the radio. It would be a secret they could share.

Alice and James returned to calling across the room. They shouted paragraphs of story and details from *How Does it Work?*. When Alice complained she could not quite hear the radio,

James sent it sailing towards her, over the three empty beds between them, as a kind of high-flying gift. But the radio fell short of its target and crashed just below Alice's bed. She saw its plastic case split open into two neat halves, and its coppery and silvery components, broken and revealed. At this point both children began to cry. In the cohesion of their little world, in reverence for the orange plastic box that was their symbol of modern magic, they heartily wailed. No grey-haired nurse came running to strike or reprove them. So they each made the most of their intelligent woe, finding in their tears an approximate expression of all that their illness, and their closeness, and their mean separation, had meant.

*

In the supermarket, at the checkout, a north African woman of extraordinary beauty was passing Alice's groceries across the scanning machine. She appeared bored and exhausted and did not look at her customers. Alice had had this job once, as a student, part time. She understood why a woman might wish to serve in this way, immured, aloof, offering no courtesy. When she announced the charge and accepted the money, she still did not look up; something burdensome weighed on her, something more than just tiredness. Numbers appeared and disappeared in small rectangular frames, black as death. The cash register slid open, sighed and retreated.

In the dark Alice walked quickly, thinking once more of Stephen. She was thinking of the ways in which desire converts to torment, and of the little boy with a bicycle and a hollow heart and a deep bafflement about life, who looked into the distance and saw his father standing on a whale. She was thinking too, thinking again, about the whale-space within which she and Norah had stood. It was like being in a body made of wind; it was englobed, but unbounded; it was strewn with light. They had laughed together. The day had been sunny and bright. Their enmity had dropped away and they had felt the blessedness of standing in bones.

Untechnical things. A woman's sadness. A boy's revelation. Two sisters compelled by nothing more than what the ocean had cast up and left behind.

*

Of all the day-to-day systems that categorise and contain, the most remorseless and omnipresent is the commercial bar code. Too much raw data circulates among us. There is a maddening variety to the products of our age. So in 1952, two graduate students from the Drexel Institute, in Philadelphia, USA, invented the bar code. It had the beauty of a hieroglyph and the forensic power of a Holmes, and it ordered everlastingly the consumerist chaos. As products swept across red scanners, there was the triumphal electronic *ping* of a new world order. A new language of capital. A new abacus of money-making. Logical scrutability. The black column of thin lines and minuscule numbers allowed no mystification. The tally of objects was a staunch and irrepressible thing.

Unsurprisingly, the first product to be given a bar code was chewing gum: consumption with no real purpose, repetition with no end. Anti-food. Mere product. Chewable America.

*

Snow fell lightly, in the barest of flurries. In arabesques, in spirals, in small winding motions. The sky was paper white. Alice opened her mouth and caught snowflakes on her tongue as they passed. There was this insubstantiality to the natural things in the world, of which snow was exemplary. There were sparrows, bare trees. A starkness to things urban. European

46

winter was so unlike an Australian winter. Here greyness pervaded and a low-ceilinged sky. Stone buildings consolidated the monotonal chill.

As she wrote each day about the objects of modern life, those things wired, lit, automatic and swift, Alice began also to be overcome by memory and dream. Anomalous thoughts occured unbidden, flashes of her past, incursions of primitive intuition. It was not that she wished not to care about such things, it was that, in this context, they were so unexpected. She felt riven, dissipated. In the fretted light of small cafés Alice could be seen scribbling away, a cup of coffee before her, trying to render the world in prose, trying to unlock with words the complicated insides of things, coiled and secret as any radio, flung long ago against authority in the isolation ward of a hospital.

Alice had begun thinking about her father. He had grown up in another age, before television, before astronauts, and had been apprenticed at the age of twelve to an electrician. He was a serious boy, very quiet and respectful, with a mass of black hair, black eyes and olive skin, so that throughout his life he would be variously mistaken as Italian, Aboriginal, Arabic or just plain foreign. His name suited him: *Frederick Black*. It was the name of a man solid and self-assured.

Fred lived in a mining town and from the age of sixteen was employed underground. In the gold mines electricians were necessarily esteemed; the world of perpetual dark, treacherous, base, needed labour that enabled men to conquer the earth. There was the heaving of dirt, the creation of tunnels and the blasting-away of rock, but there was also illumination, strings of yellow bulbs and lamps on hard hats. There were electric-powered machines that assisted muscles and saved men's lives. Fred was a genius with wires, the other blokes said. He worked his trade honourably and with unassuming diligence. He was a good electrician. Blackie, they called him. Blackie the lights man.

After a cave-in at the mine, in which seven miners were entombed, Fred decided to quit. He had been in the rescue party, trailing caged lamps attached to noisy generators, showing others the way, finding crevices, weak spots, finally scrabbling with his bare hands in the piles of fallen rocks, trying to offer breath, trying to break through. He swore that he heard a human voice, a moan, perhaps, sifting like a secret through the dusty darkness, and the other men, persuaded, dug on their knees beside him. But when at last they recovered the bodies, not one man had survived. Fred moved the lamp over their suffocated faces. They were coated with crushed earth and had become effigies of men, clay and quartz. They did not look peaceful; they just looked *gone*. One man, Jacko, was Fred's close mate. The Jacko before him was curled, like a child asleep. He had rubble covering the length of his body and a layer of rough dirt on his face. It was clear that he had cried. There were encrustations of sand at the eyelashes and trails along the cheeks. Fred wiped his sweaty palms on the seat of his pants, as if cleaning away the deaths.

'*Gone,*' he told his mother at the kitchen table, his trembling hands clasped around a cup of brown tea.

When at twenty he finally left the mine, Fred seemed older than other men of his age. He had about him a reserve, a tentative stillness. He wired houses, now, climbing high into roofs, threading coloured wires into long wall cavities, drilling plugs, making connections, practising · the sorcery of light. Sometimes he stood on a roof just to feel the sun on his face, the intensity of daylight and the immeasurable arc of the sky.

*

Fred met his wife Pat at a Firemen's Ball. The joke was that there was not a fireman to be seen, but that other workers came every year to flirt, get drunk and kick up their heels. She was a sandy-coloured woman, with large green eyes. She wore a corsage of wilted orange rosebuds set high on her chest. They were bound with silver paper and matched the tones of her dress. Fred saw in this woman some reflective aspect of his own sense of enclosure. He spat on his fingers and smoothed his hair before he approached her. When they danced he could smell her eau de Cologne, 4711; he leaned his face against her warm curls and wanted never to leave. He proposed that night. They were married three months later. The wedding photographs show a thin dark man, standing awkwardly in his hired suit, a little aslant, and a woman in a full satin gown, looking like a movie star. She had a netted veil and imitation pearls at her throat; she seemed double the groom's size and absolutely vertical. It would be ten years before they would have a child, then a second daughter would arrive, two years on.

They moved to the city, believing, as working-class people often did, that within the city are arcane routes of enlargement and success, that there are enhancements of fortune and exemptions of failure, that work is more easily come by, that prospects for children are better. They bought a weatherboard house in a neglected inner suburb – its poor eastern edge, near the bend of the wide river – and settled there, content, amazed each anniversary to have found one another, an electrician and a shop assistant, folded together, fitting, neat as ironed pleats, matched as a plug within an electrical socket.

The stories of their parents that come to children carry an amber glow. Alice and Norah knew of the mining accident, and the dance, and had seen photographs of their parents' married life before they were born. Each loved the history that inhered there, in those flat parcels of time. The oldest image they had seen was one of their grandmother holding their father as a baby. She had a plait wound around her head, and clutched him against her, a chubby bright fellow, his eyes alight, switched on. It was a definitive image of maternal pride. It conveyed in gesture alone the emotional sequence that enabled Fred Black, in the future, to hold his daughters likewise, entrusted, adored, buoyed against the drear weightiness and downwards tendency of life. Both Alice and Norah appeared in such photographs, their feet kicked up out of frothy dresses. If it was yesterday represented, it was also temporal defeat and mysterious futurity.

*

When Alice returned from the library it was still early, but already dark. She carried her plastic shopping bags, heavy with wine, cheese, vegetables, chocolate, and saw Stephen standing once again near the shadowy doorway, waiting. Alice felt a moment of panic, but Stephen raised his hand in a policeman's stop sign, as if by some new understanding he detected her alarm, and wished at once to calm her.

'It's OK,' he said. 'I've come to tell you I'm leaving. I'm going home to Australia.'

Alice stood still, unsure. Under the streetlamp Stephen appeared gaunt and pitiable. He rubbed his gloveless hands vigorously in the cold night air.

'It's true. I leave Thursday.' Then he added: 'You can come to the airport, if you want.'

Stephen's manner had changed. He spoke without demand. He said he wanted to apologise. His face was a white screen, as if he wore a reflecting visor.

Alice invited Stephen into her studio. In the blinking-on of the light it looked barer and messier than usual, books and papers scattered, discarded clothes on the floor.

'Have you eaten?' she asked.

They shared a meal, that night, of vegetables and rice, Indian style. They drank wine and ate dark chocolate studded with hazelnuts. Stephen was polite and subordinate. He hung his hands between his legs and stared at them intently.

'I've decided,' he declared at last, 'to spend a while with my mother. I think it's time we really got to know one another.' He took a large swallow of wine. 'She's ill,' he added. 'I heard just three days ago. It was like being pulled back to flesh after this . . .' he paused, 'this ontological insecurity.'

Here Stephen offered what Alice thought of as his philosopher's smile.

'I'm sorry,' he said softly. 'I haven't been myself.' He smiled again, more wanly. 'He never beat her, you know. He was just a useless drunk. I think that she loved him. She told me once that he played the fiddle as a young man. She met him in a pub, playing the fiddle. Something happened to his shoulder, some kind of industrial accident, and when he couldn't play, he drank instead. Sounds soppy, I know, but that's how it was.

'He coulda beena contenda,' Stephen added, in a Bronx-sounding accent. 'He coulda beena contenda in the fiddlin' game.'

'You're drunk,' said Alice.

'No, just thinking about them. About her. How she managed living with him, and alone. She was thirty-four when she left. That day she wore a blue dress with a print of tiny white flowers. I have a glossy image, like one from an advertisement, of her dress rippling around her knees as she strides out the door. It's just an image, of course; I didn't see her leave. But it has stayed with me, vividly, all these years . . . We never really know our parents, do we?'

*

Alice dreamed that night that she saw her mother standing on a whale. Pat waved and looked happy. Her hair blew in a bronze flag. The sun was shining. Somewhere, far off, there was the faint sound of a fiddle.

In the morning Alice considered her seizure of Stephen's tale – unconscious as it was – and could make little sense of it all. In what happens between people, she reflected, there are these transmigrations, these episodes of smudged experience, in which the containers of memory and story become weak and permeable. Images leak like smoke. Emotions. Chance utterances. Rudimentary threads of being float outwards, and reattach. Fibres of some counterlife, that which we make through others, join like the ganglia of an unlocatable, interstitial intelligence. We confederate. We are many. We carry others' stories. As she stood beneath the shower with her eyes closed, the dream was still unravelling. There was the ocean, or a river. There was shuddery wind. There was a sound like the roar of a fire, then her smiling mother disappeared. Alice opened her eyes, overcome by sexual longing. She watched rivulets of water slide over her breasts. She admired her own body and wanted it held. That she was so taken by this moment – 'pulled back to flesh,' Stephen had said – struck her as both surprising and oddly reasonable.

4

The night Stephen flew out, Alice accompanied him to Charles de Gaulle Airport. They sat together on the train, his bulky luggage shivering between them, finding little to say. Dark rain spattered the glass, sliding horizontally across the window. Mysterious signatures of neon flashed and departed. Hot pinks. Toxic greens. Pathological yellows. It was as if, outside the train, the world had converted to a system of electrical communication, wrought by arrangements of light answering light, in gaudy display. Alice imagined people with transmitters affixed to their heads, like miners' helmets, beaming statements, questions, existential cries, their faces lacquered with bright responses.

Stephen was both distracted and preoccupied.

'I'm resigned,' he said. 'I was only staying in Europe to see you, and *ya broka ma heart.*' The accent was execrable. Stephen knew it.

He pulled his overcoat more tightly closed and rewound his scarf. 'At least it will be warm,' he said absent-mindedly.

Alice put her arm around him, but he shrugged her off. It was like being underwater, this dismal parting. Stephen spoke like one who had forgotten the purpose of words. He was remote, agitated, no doubt waiting for a sign, some kind of message or promise of reconnection. The atmosphere was

moist and heavy, the light a subaqueous beige. The faces of
the passengers to the airport were bleached and closed, like
deep-sea creatures. Alice had noticed this before, this aquar-
ium quality of public transport, the peculiar air, the dulling
effects of suspension. There was a fatigue in such spaces, a
quality of spiritual surrender. Someone might die here and
go unnoticed. There might be a silent atrocity. A casual act
of abuse.

When they reached the platform at the station Stephen
wanted immediately to part.

'Let's leave it here,' he said abruptly.

He took Alice's hand and kissed her fingertips. Then he
turned with his heavy luggage and did not pause or look back.
Alice watched him step onto the escalator, like a man sucked
upwards, a man who had entered a sinister wartime movie,
something by Orson Welles, or Kubrick, perhaps, and disappear
into the vast steel cavern of the terminal. She was left there,
by herself, as if she was the spurned one. Totalitarian announcements from a loudspeaker commanded her attention. Crowds
pushed past her, heading in the opposite direction. Alice looked
at the lime-green electronic clock and the list of lit stations.
Then she walked to the other side of the platform and boarded
the train back to Paris. She had not even told him her dream,
or said goodbye.

*

The history of mechanised hearts, *wrote Mr Sakamoto*,
is a melancholy history. The heart is an organ not
easily governed at the best of times. William Harvey,
who was born in Kent, England in 1578 and studied at
the universities of Cambridge and Padua, conducted
enough dissections of human and animal corpses to
refute the commonplace idea that food was converted

into blood by the liver. He suggested instead –
somewhat scandalously at the time – that blood was
pumped from the heart throughout the body and then
returned and recirculated. Harvey stood back from his
gory investigative procedures, covered with the
controversial stuff-of-life that had once passed inside
a human heart, and knew for certain the function of
valves and veins, and that his esteemed mentor,
Hieronymus Fabricius, was wrong in supposing that
arteries were the origin of the pulse. His theory was
published in 1628.

The heart-pump identification did not change the
minds of anyone but physicians. The rest of the world
continued to attribute capacities and functions,
generally bizarre and mostly wide-ranging. Half-
truths and one-and-a-half-truths, garbled theories
and romantic miscalculations – all contributed to
swell the heart to abnormal size, pumped up by
symbolism. By the nineteenth century, scientists
began again to attend to its physical properties: two
British physiologists, having recorded, with modest
purpose, the electrical currents of a frog's heart,
decided immodestly to apply this technology to
humans. The electrocardiogram, as it was named in
1887, recorded the heart's phases, beats and delays. It
noted atrial stimulation and ventricular depolarisa-
tion. It monitored, let us be frank, inner secrets.
Tamed by electricity, it was only a matter of time
before pacemakers, batteries and artificial hearts
together intervened to heal and control. But this
paradox persists: although the heart has succumbed
to exposure and regulation, to electromechanical
jiggery-pokery, it continues stubbornly to accrete

nonmaterial accessories. Deforming meanings enlarge and empower it. It pounds on, as it were, at 100,000 beats a day, 100,000 lub Dub, lub Dub, lub Dub, lub Dub, but it is still a site of the greatest obscurity. Lost or found, sometimes torn or broken, sometimes wholly unknowable.

William Harvey, bless his soul, had the faith of the lover. He saw the chestnut-haired Elizabeth Browne, daughter of one of the Queen's physicians, reading a book beneath a shady tree. Light fell on the side of her face and across the open pages of her book. He felt his heart leap within him, stir, and strike more boldly. When they married it was still thus. He was overexcited. His heart was crazy – boom-boom – struck by love.

*

With Stephen gone, Alice was calmer and better able to work. She spent her days inward-turned, reading and writing. The weather gradually became warmer, and with it her antipodean self seemed to revive: she took long walks across bridges and along the banks of the river; she visited and left churches, a tourist, merely; she eavesdropped on conversations and sat alone in blustery parks reading flapping English newspapers. She was entering a state of dematerialisation. The rowdy city that had first seemed so pressurising and insistent, now withdrew, faded, as if she too were faded and had no solid body to press upon. There was static in the air, a kind of quivering charge. Radio waves, microwaves, the Big Bang resounding. Alice felt she had been parachuted in, but not quite landed, so that she hung above the earth, an inflated dome shadowing her, recording and surveying with cunning intent. Below, the world of children, lapdogs, men having arguments, roller skaters, wanderers and lovers on Pont Neuf, continued with its own intrinsic purpose and animation. Camus had said in his *Carnets* that the lives of others appear always, from the outside, to have a completion our own dismally lacks. Only when we understand this as a projection — that other lives, too, are unclosed and contingent — do we approach maturity. Alice felt immature. She felt that she was a spy in the cold.

One day Alice fell asleep during an afternoon organ concert at Notre-Dame, and woke from the remnants of an erotic dream, spliced and impersonal as pornography. The friction of thighs, a lubricious kiss, insertions, retractions, the spill of energy. Her own participation, her own complicity. A trail of words drifted back: *spiritualisation, secularisation, sexualisation.* Something shifted outside, a single cloud perhaps, and sunlight began streaming through the western rose window, beginning as white, then dispersing into colours. People sitting in the pews were all of a sudden spotted: pink, blue, yellow and green. Their faces bore a sheen and they looked blessed, distinguished. It was an ordinary phenomenon that, in this heightened space and contrived luminosity, carried a sense of election, of privileged moments.

Alice watched as people in the cathedral began to notice the special effect, and then to exclaim and raise their voices. Cameras of all shapes and sizes appeared from nowhere. Within seconds everyone sitting in the section beneath the window light seemed to be photographing, or being photographed. The stained-glass colours dispersed in a hundred white flashes, evacuated by technology, destroyed by tiny machines. A prism reversed. 'Smile!' Alice heard beside her, and an over-large American family of four lined up to be snapshot.

Only later, when she was slowly walking home, feeling

vaguely depressed, did Alice wonder if her face too had been coloured, if she had been a yellow or a blue, tinted as if by moonlight, or if, for a fleeting instant, she had been a rose.

*

'Like a cradle, gently rocking.' Where was that line from?

Alice was returning from a few days' break in Chartres, having submitted to her inexplicable fascination for cathedrals. The train rocked into the night, its passengers embraced in a maternal rhythm. Alice had been drowsily watching her own ghost on the surface of the window, seized by the obscure despondency of trains, when she heard music from some-where, possibly a transistor radio. John Lennon's mournful voice, posthumous and unearthly, floated towards her, down the full length of the carriage:

> 'Instant karma's gonna get you
> Gonna knock you right on the head
> You better get yourself together
> Pretty soon you're gonna be dead
> What in the world you thinking of
> Laughing in the face of love
> What on earth you tryin' to do
> It's up to you, yeah you.'

The man sitting opposite Alice opened his eyes and smiled. '"Instant Karma",' he said. 'This song is called "Instant Karma".'

He was a Japanese man of about seventy-five. He had backward-swept grey hair and a look of sleepy composure.

'I was once in love with Yoko Ono. Her boldness. Her art. Her international life.' He removed his glasses and rubbed his eyes with his fists. An enormous wristwatch glinted in the dim light of the train. 'In the sixties, of course.'

Alice liked his smile. And the unexpected intimacy of his confession.

'In that song,' he went on without prompting, 'in the video of that song, Yoko Ono is brindforded.'

Alice could not quite make out the last word. Brindforded? Ah, blindfolded.

'Blindfolded,' she found herself repeating, as if correcting his accented pronunciation. She was momentarily aware that he might consider her rude or pedantic.

'Just so,' he repeated. 'Brindforded.'

The words oscillated between them, rocking as the train rocked, catching their national inflections.

The man smiled again. 'Sakamoto,' he added, with a half-bow of his body.

Alice leaned forward and extended her hand. 'Black, Alice Black.'

'The colour?'

'The colour.' (Was it a colour or an absence?)

They shook hands, meeting in the small memory room the song had opened. Then they listened together until the end:

> 'Well we all shine on,
> Like the moon and the stars and the sun,
> Yeah we all shine on
> On and on and on on and on . . .'

Mr Sakamoto introduced himself: an independent scholar, from Nagasaki, writing a biography, he said, of Alexander Graham Bell, the inventor of the telephone. (The word sounded like 'terror-phone'.)

'The telephone', Mr Sakamoto said, leaning forward, 'is the most metaphysical of all technologies. It reveals and it effaces, it is fulsome and forsaken, it enfolds and estranges.'

Alice listened with delight to this little speech. It was as if they shared a minority language. Or harboured a hidden secret. Or a freakish enthusiasm.

'Yes,' she said. 'I am writing, among other things, about the extraordinary existence of the telephone. I am writing a book – trying to write a book – about modern things: Xerox machines, neon lights, photography, astronauts.'

This work sounded meretricious, almost childish, as she announced it. But Mr Sakamoto beamed approval.

'So we must be friends!' he declared. 'We *must* be friends! I am so pleased to meet you, Black, Alice Black.'

Alice liked the sound of her name with the l's abraded.

It was such an easy meeting. Friends are an intersection, a route back to the world. Alice could not have foreseen that this Japanese man, this man, she would discover, who was sixty-eight, not seventy-five, from the city of Nagasaki, would greet her with such openness and affinity that it would be impossible not to befriend him. He too seemed responsive to something in Alice's manner – not just her project, but the earnestness of her isolation, the dedication to an intellectual cause, the pleasure in supposing the usual arcane, the familiar compelling. If there is a magnetic aspect to sensibility it is evident in friendships that arise from these merest conversations and shreds of sentences, talks that align particles of self in a sudden, energised correspondence.

Alice remembered at some stage that she had seen the video clip of 'Instant Karma'. Yoko Ono wore a kind of bandage across her eyes, thick and white, as if she were not simply blindfolded, but wounded, or even blind. There were words on cards and peace-symbol armbands, and Lennon, with a thin beard and a lazy tambourine. In front of the band, dancers were bobbing arhythmically, under strobe lights. They wore Carnaby Street gear and had fixed expressions. Alice had no idea what year this performance was from: it was something lodged in her girlhood, something as almost forgotten and as lost as a beached whale. Mr Sakamoto fell back to sleep. Alice watched him rest his face in his hand, arrange his pullover as a pillow against the cold surface of the window, and then re-enter his own seclusion. He looked calm, she thought. Wise. When they arrived at the station he awoke with a jolt and was instantly communicative.

'We must talk, Alice Black, about this world of modern things. This buzzing world.'

Mr Sakamoto gestured around him at the hubbub of the train station, with everyone rushing helter-skelter for the exits. He offered Alice a name card from his wallet and wrote on it the phone number of his hotel. Since she did not have a card, Alice scribbled her name and email address on a slip of paper.

'Soon,' he said, reaching to shake her hand once again.

Mr Sakamoto turned into the crowd, walked a few paces and then looked back. He waved extravagantly, with a kind of Florentine flourish. Alice waved back in a huge reply. They were already mimicking each other, already blithe in their friendship.

*

Dear Alice,

Forgive me for taking so long to answer your letter; things here have been getting on top of me.

It's been a particularly hot summer – yesterday was 40, oppressive, and everyone was grumpy and short-tempered in the heat – and then there is all this talk of going to war with Iraq, which seems madness on almost any pretext. I fear – what do they call it? – the 'collateral damage' of women and children and the ghastly sense that superpowers will once again play out their posturing antipathies by bombing the shit out of people they can't see. And that it will go on for years and years, with poor and powerless people invisibly suffering. Michael and I have joined an anti-war group, but it's looking inevitable. The government here are slavish appeasers; they want the approval of Uncle Sam at any price.

The other upsetting issue at the moment is the treatment of refugees. Bloody 'border protection', is what they're calling it. The detention centres are nightmarish and there are still children in there, held behind razor wire. We are lobbying for the release of the children – since neither party, as you know, will close down the centres – but getting nowhere fast. I'd planned to go on a trip to the desert, to visit one of the centres, but have had to cancel for other reasons. So Michael and I send phone cards and toys, but we're not sure if anything we send is actually given to the inmates. Australia distresses me, this barricade mentality, this fear of the 'illegal' refugees, this rightist neo-nationalism. Perhaps you're sensible to be away, overseas, thinking of other things.

I saw Stephen last week, for a cup of coffee. He is still in love with you, and in a bit of a mess, frankly, but seems to have made progress in getting to know his mother – who has cancer, by the way, as half the world seems to have. He said she has spoken to him of her childhood in an orphanage in England, how she was 'shipped out' to Australia with fantasy promises, how she met his father in a pub somewhere, playing the fiddle. Stephen seems pleased that she's talking but says it's because she's dying. I told him not everyone who has cancer dies of it. He has picked up some part-time university teaching, and says he will stay at least six months, then consider his options. He'd love to hear from you, if you're inclined to write.

Michael and the children are fine. Michael has a job on a community housing project in the northern suburbs, which takes up all of his time. But he seems pleased to be working in the public sector again and is finally believing that architecture is a worthwhile profession. David is still not talking much (unlike Helen, who chatters incessantly), but seems cheerful enough and is obsessed with Thomas the Tank Engine. Helen is actually taller than her brother, and strangers always assume she's the older child. She has a tendency to throw objects when she becomes frustrated, and at the moment David has a nasty cut on his temple from a hurtled block. I still love it when they're asleep – this sounds terrible, I know – but they are so beautiful and at peace (and quiet!) and I have time to read or paint. Mum's been over a bit lately, helping out. She and Dad ask me to remind you to write more often. Both are doing as well as can be expected after the operation. Dad moves more slowly now, but is otherwise recovered and back to his gardening.

As to the whale, why do you assume, Alice, that you're the only one ever to remember these things? Of course I remember it. We were in trouble for wandering off, but still felt elated at our discovery. I too remember how we stood in the skeleton shapes and felt the mystery of it, and the charm, and realised that we'd stumbled upon something marvellous. The spinal bone was left behind when we returned to the city. Dad tried to fit it in the car, but it was just too large, and too oddly shaped. So we left it at the front door of the shack, festooned with dried seaweed and decorated with pretty shells. It may still be there, for all I know. Or someone may have claimed it, or sold it, or taken it for a garden. We weren't always fighting, were we? There were these occasions of joint experience and pleasure.

How is your work going? I have none to speak of – apart from mothering – but am optimistic I will return one day to full-time painting. Michael doesn't think so, but I'm determined to prove him wrong.

Take care, big sister. Send me a cute Parisian story about your life. And thank you for the wooden toys. At the moment they're on a shelf, a little like art objects, but the children will grow, I'm sure, to see their attraction.

Yours,
Norah

*

Across the sky, superimposed, were the vapour trails of jet planes. Alice stood on windy Pont Marie, tilted her head, and looked up at the white lattice trails of international air travel. She was vaguely shocked that the territory of the sky could be so marked by transit, but also thrilled at the design, at the modern writ so ethereally. Below her, tourists passed beneath the bridge on a broad open boat. It appeared sturdy, like a workers' vessel, having the look of faux antiquity. The river was jade-coloured, rippled. Alice saw someone on the deck pause and take her photograph, as if she were a Frenchwoman-on-a-bridge, a genuine spectacle. She waved, and the photographer looked up, embarrassed, and turned immediately away.

Alice was walking to meet her new friend, Mr Sakamoto. They were to lunch at a small bistro on the Left Bank, and would talk, he said emphatically, about this buzzing world. Alice moved through the cobbled streets with an air of anticipation, as if he were forty years younger, and her secret assignation.

Mr Sakamoto would raise his glass of red wine.

'The difficulty with celebrating modernity,' he declared, 'is that we live with so many persistently unmodern things. Dreams, love, babies, illness. Memory. Death. And all the natural things. Leaves, birds, ocean, animals. Think of your Australian kangaroo,' he added. 'The kangaroo is truly unmodern.'

Here he paused and smiled, as if telling himself a joke. 'And sky. Think of sky. There is nothing modern about the sky.'

'Vapour trails,' responded Alice, pretending to miss his point.

5

Hiroshi Sakamoto was born in Nagasaki, in 1934, into a wealthy family who lived on the south-eastern hillside of the city, over-looking the harbour. Below, they could see ships of many nations on the turquoise water and the day-to-day arriving and leaving of vessels of commerce and trade. Further out, there were small fishing boats dotted around the bay; these too swept in and out, regular and irregular as the weather permitted. The view extended to promontories, sky, to the horizon of the ocean. They could see rain approaching in blue veils and clouds mass and unfurl. It was expansive and mobile; it was a view that encouraged journeying. Up and down the steep slopes of the hillside moved figures, sedan chairs and heavy carts, so that one could believe one sat high upon a world of relentless labour.

Hiroshi's father, Osamu, had inherited a fortune, being the only heir to a centuries-old sake business. The raking and cool-ing of rice, the smell of fermentation, the rituals of purifying water and the appeasement of spirits, these were all encoded so thoroughly in Osamu as a child that no one would imag-ine that his interests would turn to the production of steel. Although he maintained the sake business, almost purely for sentimental reasons and the tremor of nostalgic pleasure whenever he smelled rice at its final stage and saw women bent with large fans above steaming trays, he was seduced by industrial manufacture and the intricacy of machines. In the late 1920s he visited America with a translator in tow, and saw there the production-line assembly of motorised vehicles, welders and machinists contriving the engines of aircraft, and women with nimble hands, each producing a little component of a Wurlitzer wireless. Although he found America crass, ugly and with no civic decorum, when he returned to Nagasaki Sakamoto-san told his associates: 'I have seen the future, and it works,' and set about establishing a chain of factories in the Nagasaki prefecture. By 1934, his premises produced both the tiny cogs of watches and the girders for a bridge, and metal items of assorted shapes and sizes in between, some for the Mitsubishi dockyards, some for the munitions factories.

Hiroshi had two older sisters, Sachiko and Mihoko, who doted on their younger brother and were clever and witty. They attended an exclusive girls' school in the centre of the city, at which they were taught English and French, as well as traditional academic studies and female accomplishments. Hiroshi remembers his sisters chattering trilingually, making jokes and exchanging confidences in a plait of languages. Sometimes, in the space of one or two sentences, Sachiko and Mihoko shifted linguistic registers, so that no one knew exactly what they were talking about, and Hiroshi was often frustrated to the point of tears when he could not follow their secretive, erratic conversations.

When he was six his father employed two private tutors – a Japanese scholar, Masa Tanaka, almost eighty, who was a famous practitioner of the art of *haiku*, and a young man from Manchester, England, who was not particularly scholarly, but adored his own language with singular devotion. Harold O'Toole was twenty-six years old, had startling blond hair, and fell almost at once in love with Sachiko, who had turned seventeen the week he arrived. Hiroshi detected his foreign tutor's divided attentions and strove to excel, anxious to impress the young man with his English language fluency and his penchant for difficult vocabulary. By the time he was eleven, in 1945, Hiroshi was reading classic English novels and adopting regional accents as a form of play – although still not quite commanding the pronunciation of 'l'. Harold O'Toole – who had been protected from internment during the war by the wealth of the Sakamotos – was still love-struck by Sachiko, but by then she was interested in a young biology teacher, a Christian, who worked at the Chinzei middle school. Only when Hiroshi was an adult did he learn from his mother that Mihoko had been in love with Harold O'Toole, and that this mismatch of feeling, this mis-crossing of desires, had caused the family much worry and distress.

Of the day in August 1945, when the world changed, changed utterly, Mr Sakamoto disclosed very little. Alice must not be offended, he said; he had never told his wife or two adult daughters the details of his experience. The outline was simply that he and his mother had been saved, but that the rest of the family had perished. Almost everyone he knew had perished. Sachiko and Mihoko had perished. His father. Mr O'Toole. The biology teacher in Chinzei middle school. Almost 74,000 people in the explosion alone. His Japanese tutor, who at the time of the explosion had been in the mountains meditating by a stream, survived, but wished he hadn't and committed suicide two weeks after the blast. Poetry, said Mr Sakamoto, was no longer possible.

The child Hiroshi and his mother moved to Tokyo, where she had relatives. When Tadeo, his mother's brother, returned from the war, they all lived together in a small apartment near a bombed-out suburb. At length Uncle Tadeo discovered

Osamu's overseas bank accounts, and the existence of two remaining factories in Honshu, and the makeshift family, bleak with grief, moved to a larger dwelling in a better area.

Hiroshi was a restless young man who could settle to nothing and was afraid of attachment. He entered an intellectual world of remote theorems and calculations, and at one time entertained the idea – somewhat vengefully – of becoming a theoretical physicist. But some 'perversity', he said, intuitively prevailed, so that in post-war Japan, when others turned to pragmatism and the business of reconstruction, he found himself reading *haiku*, and English novels and European poetry in translation. He felt like a being from another planet. In Tokyo, cacophonous with the manufacture of new buildings and the incessant clang of metal, he lost himself in the quiet domain of seventeen syllables, the make-believe lives of raven-haired heroines and country gentlemen, and the storm and stress of faraway poetic emotions. Often he dreamed of his sisters, and his father, and of people now gone. In his dreams his sisters always spoke in a language he could not understand and he would wake himself, weeping.

After an uneventful few years at university, Hiroshi began travelling. His uncle indulged him, funding his nephew's whims, while at the same time sending gently hectoring letters about the need to find a profession and accumulate wealth. On a pretext of scholarship, Hiroshi found himself settling for a time in Edinburgh, a city he admired for its unusual combination of stately complacency and rough-at-the-edges commitment to life. The Scots, declared Mr Sakamoto, are a people given to mischievous intelligence and the cultivation of irony. At a bookshop he met and fell in love with Clare MacDougall, whom he had first encountered sitting in lilac shadow in the classics section, on a small oak stool, reading a battered second-hand edition of Homer. She was attracted to his foreignness, his upright posture, the neat pert bows with which he greeted her, his low respectful voice; he, to what he perceived as her explicit sameness: she had black eyes and hair, a flat face and a small nose, and she read with a transported intensity he immediately recognised as his own. They courted in the usual way – walks up to the castle, drinks at the pub, the occasional swift kiss in a wynd or on the doorstep of her home – but perhaps both knew it would come to nothing. Clare's two brothers called Hiroshi a 'Jap', and treated him with vicious and undisguised contempt. Her parents were appalled – and told her so – that she would 'walk out with a yellow man', for all the world to see. Not much irony there, Clare had commented. When Clare refused to stop seeing Hiroshi, her brothers beat her. She arrived at their dinner date with a broken cheekbone and a blue bruised face, and tearfully announced that it was all too difficult. In the candlelight of the café, she looked like a young woman ruined. Hiroshi had seen enough of wounded bodies to want not to be the cause of any more, so he made a quick decision and left Edinburgh the next day. They wrote letters to each other for almost three years. When Clare announced her engagement to a man working in the Bank of Scotland, the letters between them abruptly ceased.

Against his uncle's advice and wishes, Hiroshi returned to Nagasaki. With a portion of his inheritance he purchased a sake company – one still teetering on the edge of oblivion after the death of most of its workers in 1945 – believing he could remake the family tradition and honour his father. Under his control for six months, the sake business was a moderate success; however, Hiroshi found he had no feeling or instinct for the processes and practices that had so occupied his family over generations, and in the end appointed a manager and returned to his books. He watched the gradual redevelopment of the city of Nagasaki – the tram tracks, the schools, the stores and harbourside – but no longer felt any connection to the place he had grown up in. Every building was new and unrecognisable, and the hammering, hauling, carting, scaffolding, seemed to continue both day and night, even now, fifteen years after the unmentionable event. The population who had remained included many burns victims, gaunt figures with melted skin and woeful eyes. They appeared everywhere as a kind of indictment. Hiroshi felt obliged to stay, but hated being there; he hated coming across a burned person and the reminder of what cannot be repaired.

Only the view of the harbour remained essentially the same. There were more ships, these days, but the water was a clear turquoise blue and the view across to the shimmering horizon was, as ever, transfixing. The sky seemed larger now, and the hills more steep, especially since there were still areas of deforestation and small young trees. Hiroshi stood at the front of his wooden house – built in the traditional style – and stared for hours at the ocean and the sky, at the forces that pull the rain and the clouds, at the screen of colours that swapped back and forth the day and the night with what seemed such perpetually meaningless insistence.

At length, desperately lonely, Hiroshi noticed a pretty young woman of a good family who was not Clare Mac-Dougall, but whom he believed eventually he could love. Mie was a small woman who seemed delicate to the point of fragility, and Hiroshi felt tenderly protective towards her. He found himself bending over her, looking at the top of her head, then her face would upturn and she would smile at him directly. It was an offering, a benevolence, amid the city's waste. When they married, he thought she looked like a doll. Perhaps he had been too long abroad, but the white face powder and the heavy kimono and the elaborate decorations in her hair, presented his bride as an ornamental stranger. During the ceremony Hiroshi had irrepressible misgivings, but decided then and there that he would be a devoted husband. His mother cried. Uncle Tadeo looked pleased. It was a late spring morning and the cherry blossoms were at last beginning to fall. Loose petals flew in the air like snowflakes. He was reminded that there was lightness, as well as gravity, that there are presences in the wind, unassuming, and precious possibilities.

Mie had two daughters, Akiko and Haruko, and Hiroshi rejoiced. In his children he was healed. In his children there was a future, and the swapping of day and night at the end of the ocean was now the meaningful marker of their daily growth. Akiko and Haruko were cheerful and without burned history. They laughed at the slightest pretext and were inclusively sociable. Hiroshi read them storybooks and bought them sweets and electronic toys. He liked nothing more than to walk along the street holding hands, one daughter on each side, watching their linked shadows, a wobbly triangle, proceed in silhouette over the earth before them. When they both went to school he found it difficult to adjust. He would wait at the school entrance to walk them home, and then become annoyed when they wanted to close off and watch television. He looked at their backs, crouched in the flickering light. He thought often of Harold O'Toole and Masa Tanaka, and still believed in the superiority of words over images.

Mie died when her oldest daughter was twelve. Her leukemia was probably the consequence of radiation exposure; in any case her death fell over the household like radioactive ash. Akiko became sullen and withdrawn and as an adult would later suffer depressive episodes and acts of self-harm. Haruko was more resilient, but still altered by the loss and robbed of her unselfconscious delight. It was she to whom

Hiroshi secretly felt closer, but in truth he could talk to no one of what Mie had come to mean, of her quiet solidity, of her offer of redemption. His mother came to live with them, but she was by then withered and ill, and Hiroshi feared that his children would meet with a second death. When she died just two months later, he felt at the point of collapse. And it was his mother's death, not Mie's, that threatened to derange him.

It was then 1972 and Hiroshi was at last experiencing the grief of 1945. It was as if he had held it under control for all these years, just to have it now bubble up to the surface, released through the fine jagged fissures a single death might cause. He ceased eating and sleeping. When he slept for what seemed only a moment, he was engulfed by nightmares. When he was awake he encountered long-ago visions. For the sake of his daughters, he pretended stability, but Hiroshi was shaken daily by the deep seismic forces of what had never been confronted or resolved. One day Uncle Tadeo visited and took the girls with him back to Tokyo, to stay for a time with their relatives. Hiroshi spent four weeks in a clinic by the ocean where, chemically sedated, he entered another kind of time and began in dread negation to sleep. It was the drowned sleep of drugs, it was obliteration. Outside his window the water swelled and subsided, swelled and subsided, a truly dull repetition. A dozen dead oceans, Mr Sakamoto said, a hard rain. Hiroshi discovered that the clinic was exclusively for *Hibakusha*, for atomic bomb survivors. There were people with decades-old burns scars and conspicuous injuries, but there were also people like him, who bore no visible scar at all, but who had seen what was unassimilable and been occupied by loss.

When he was reunited with his daughters, Hiroshi resumed his daily life with as much regularity as possible. He met them after school, and let them watch too much television. He prepared simple meals, and the girls began, through his poor efforts, to take an interest in cooking.

Once a week he saw a doctor from the clinic, a kindly man who shared his interest in literature and with whom he exchanged his favourite *haiku*. So Hiroshi moved again into the solace of seventeen syllables, into the space of the meticulous image and the precise meditation. He found there a nonchemical repose, an amethyst light. Drops of water, chrysanthemums, the beat of moth wings in smoky air: these noticed felicities, these forms of simple praise, reconfigured by small degrees the entire world. As he dipped the brush and created the ink characters, he felt as if old Masa Tanaka was still sitting at his side. And although his own efforts often seemed inept, he enjoyed, most of all, the task of attention, and practised *haiku* as a spiritual exercise.

Each day Uncle Tadeo spoke to him on the telephone. Hiroshi grew to cherish their quirky conversations. His uncle was more fluent and open on the telephone than face to face, and an intimacy grew between them that had not existed before. Even Hiroshi found himself whispering into the mouthpiece things he would not have been able to say directly, personal things, about Clare and Mie, childhood things, about the old Nagasaki, fearful things, about what he held within him, about his darkness, his memories, his crater of nightmares.

Once Hiroshi told Uncle Tadeo at length a dream from the night before: how he had seen Harold O'Toole, his blond hair a helmet of flame, shouting to him for water, shouting, and then screaming, screaming, and then chasing him, like a monster, dragging fire. The telling of this dream was a surrender of feeling into words. It was an unprecedented relief. It allowed Hiroshi to release into voice alone, into the unseeable chamber that lay between him and Tadeo, what had seemed physically to inhabit him, to rest corrosively within, to lock him into abstract and timeless isolation. He heard his own voice expelling phantom presences and wounding secrets. He gave up ghosts. He exhaled poisons. Gradually, too, Uncle Tadeo began to speak to his nephew of the war, telling for the first time his experiences of shame and desolation. In the wires of the telephone, in the windy space between mouths, they became father and son; they spoke the truth; they expressed their love. Their voices floated into each other, in a disincarnate embrace. Each time he put down the telephone receiver, Hiroshi felt he had been kissed.

Akiko and Haruko both had difficult experiences of adolescence. When they were little, Hiroshi had delighted in watching his daughters, with their Hello Kitty scarlet school bags, their lacy ankle socks, their fluffy hair ornaments and novelty keyrings, walking hand in hand as they entered the schoolyard. They looked decorated, happy. But in their teenage years Akiko became withdrawn and tormented, as if she had inherited her father's sadness, and Haruko took to exhibitionist forms of identity. At one stage – and to her older sister's great embarrassment – Haruko became a *ganguro*, tanning her face dark in sun-bed salons, dying her hair green, wearing an assortment of PVC and chains, and acting aggressively. Tadeo counselled patience, and said that grief takes many guises. Grief, he said, is a mysterious subtraction of the self; one then builds self again with whatever resources are available. When the sisters at last finished their schooling, both, in a new concord, entered the world of finance. They enjoyed the rigour of numbers and strict calculation. Fractions, decimal points, neat lists of figures. There was a quiet there, within numbers, a clean, stable space. Arithmetic saved them. Akiko and Haruko became independent, adult. The apartment they shared was a paradigm of neatness and order.

Hiroshi Sakamoto began travelling again, sliding in jet planes from country to country. Wherever he went he telephoned Uncle Tadeo every day, often speaking in sunlight to his uncle at night, or speaking in the night to his uncle at breakfast. The size and rotation of the planet did not interfere with their daily conversations. Words sped over mountains and rivers and ignored whole continents. Only on the telephone could Hiroshi utter his truths. Only there did he find expression and relief. At some point or other, at some foreign location, Hiroshi conceived of a project to which he wished finally to devote his skills and time. He would write a biography of Alexander Graham Bell, the Scotsman, the inventor of the telephone. His beloved Uncle Tadeo thought this a splendid idea.

6

The bistro was cramped, in the French style, with too much chunky wooden furniture, and suffused with the mingled odours of baking and cigarette smoke. Two fussy waiters in long aprons moved sideways in the narrow spaces between the tables, their plates held high. They seemed at war with each other and carried perpetual sneers.

Alice and Mr Sakamoto discussed the buzzing world. Over onion soup, trout with almonds, and chocolate mousse, they began gradually to know each other, to exchange ideas, opinions and stories. Mr Sakamoto was staying in Paris for an indefinite period, for no reason, he said, other than to revisit cherished sites and attend screenings of old movies. He was staying in a simple hotel on rue des Ecoles, just up from a small art cinema that showed only movies from the thirties, forties and fifties. So far, he had seen four comedies by Ernst Lubitsch and three police dramas in a Bogart retrospective.

'Movies? What do you think of movies?' Mr Sakamoto asked. 'Do you have movies in your book?'

'Not yet,' said Alice shyly. 'I'm still thinking about it.'

'When I was a child,' he said, 'before the catastrophe, my sisters often took me on outings to the movies. My father never quite approved, but he indulged us anyway, believing that

American cinema, in particular, was somehow culturally educative. *Mr Smith Goes to Washington*: that was one of my favourites. And anything with Gary Cooper. *Morocco, Beau Geste.* Beau had two brothers, John and Digby, and they all joined the Foreign Legion and ended up fighting Arabs in the desert. It was all about glamorous sacrifice; I found it very appealing. I suppose I wanted brothers . . . One of the scenes I remember most clearly is from early on in the movie. The three brothers are little boys and they are playing at setting up a Viking funeral. It's a noble burning. A splendid death. I remember discussing this afterwards with my English tutor, and he too liked the idea of a Viking funeral . . . For whichever of us dies first, he joked, the other will perform a Viking funeral. Then we shook hands.'

Mr Sakamoto paused in his monologue. He took a sip of wine.

'I've seen very few old movies,' Alice admitted. 'Some on TV. Some at festivals.'

'Then you must come with me. This afternoon. Lubitsch's *Ninotchka* is screening, starring Greta Garbo. How can you write on modernity if you haven't seen *Ninotchka*?'

Mr Sakamoto was smiling at her. Alice saw that this was a man of true generosity and spontaneous joy. He wiped a trace of mousse from his chin with a napkin.

'You'll love it,' he added. 'I promise.'

They agreed to meet in front of the cinema later that afternoon. Mr Sakamoto kissed Alice twice on both cheeks and again waved broadly as they parted. His post-prandial nap awaited him, he said. Alice watched as he climbed the steep street to the rue des Ecoles, with a faltering, uneven step she had not noticed before.

The weather had turned chilly and Alice hurried off in the opposite direction, winding her grey woollen scarf as she went.

She would take the Métro to the Village Voice bookshop, and buy a book. A novel. Something difficult. Something fashionable and new. Dining out had given her a spendthrift inclination.

But when Alice entered the Métro, she immediately heard below her loud, abusive shouting and a woman's high-pitched screams. The voices sounded echoic, enlarged and thick with emotion. She found herself running down the steps into cavernous yellow shadows, impelled by instinct, rushed on by fear, or adventure, or foolishness. Around the bend of the tunnel, at the foot of the tiled stairwell, a man was kicking, again and again, a woman lying prostrate before him. Other people hurried by, studiously ignoring them. A single old woman stood at a distance, remonstrating, jabbing her finger towards the man and shouting in a knotted language that was certainly not French. The couple were young and dark-haired. They had the distracted, edgy look of smack-hungry junkies. Alice hurled herself at the man, and pushed him bodily away. He stumbled backwards, for a second or two dumbfounded, but then swung at Alice, missing, and turned a wide arc in a kind of drunken reel, swearing to himself and kicking at the wall. Alice bent and lifted the woman to her feet. She was about twenty years old and had blood seeping in channels from her nose. Her eyes brimmed with tears. Her face was marbled with distress. Tendrils of damp hair clung to her cheeks. Without thinking, Alice wiped the woman's bloody nose with the end of her scarf, as if she were tending an injured child. The woman shrugged off her help and also turned away, following her abuser, with limping gait, towards the far exit.

There was a roar of noise and wind and a semi-dark smearing of outlines. Light-emitting diodes composed the time in a dangling box. The train had come and left; Alice stood numbly on the platform. The old woman, who seemed also to have missed her train, pulled at Alice's sleeve and said something reassuring. She may have been speaking in Polish, or Yiddish; in any case, it was an expression of friendship and approval. Alice nodded, submissively. The encounter with the bleeding woman had left her with a giddy anticipation of despair. Random violence, no matter how minor, had this predictable effect: the shuddering sensation of watching the concussive recoil of flesh, the general sense of a collapse of civility, the reminder, above all, of graver, sorrowful things that exist beneath the hyper-shine and fast-motion of cities. Alice smiled at the speaking woman, and they waited together, side by side, for the next underground train.

When it came, they entered the same sliding door, and sat looking at each other. The woman pulled up the sleeve of her coat. There, on her forearm, were blue tattooed numbers. The woman nodded at the numbers, then smiled sadly at Alice. She knew, Alice thought. She knew what this all meant. Alice nodded back. It was the barest of communications, a wordless understanding. Alice found herself, like an author, constructing a biography. The supposition of a life that carried a tattoo. Film footage played from somewhere. Visions pre-emptive. Photographs of disaster in hazy tones of brown. When the woman left the train before Alice she did not look back. She moved away into the crowd and was almost immediately obscured.

Arrived at the bookshop, Alice browsed without pleasure. The books conveyed both intimidation and overabundant presence. They lined up like the immense bar code of some key to all mythologies. There were new novels, in hardback, with expressionistic covers and virtuosic claims, and colourful paperbacks, each announcing a superior, unmatched talent. Tables sagged under so many new-minted words. So many leaves of meaning, so many sentences, strung together, in immoderately shiny covers. After slow deliberation, Alice bought a volume of Henry James's *Portrait of a Lady*. Although she had read it before, she felt it was a choice-against-disappointment, a choice that retrieved something swept away, rudely disintegrated, by blows struck against a young woman's body in the dark arcades of the Métro.

*

Speed perturbed and excited her. It was the penetration of vicinity, the counteraction of sensible space. Chronometers, speedometers – instruments supercharged against the desolation of the still.

When Alice was a child she liked to watch the weather report on television. Each evening, before the list of tidal figures and temperatures and barometric predictions, one of the stations showed a wide-angled prospect of the city, taken from its tallest building, looking out across the river, across bridges and highways. Eight hours were filmed and condensed to one or two minutes; this process was contrived to make heaven itself speed. Light arose and receded, clouds streamed in from the ocean, gathered and dispersed, rain filtered down in drifting, diaphanous waves, swept the screen with shadow, then disappeared in an instant. Boats and ferries on the river whisked past like apparitions, their wakes unfurling in patterns that looked like stitches sewn into the water. In the corner of the screen, barely discernible, a digital clock flicked figures with alarming swiftness, showing not time's arrow, but time's perpetual superfluity. Fleetingness. Relentlessness. Irretrievability. The film of the weather was transfixing because it was so unnatural, yet it provided the illusionist gratification, at once terrifying and beautiful, that one might speed up time, that one might push nature faster, that there was a perspective, somewhere, somewhere up very high, of panoramic relativity.

Norah also loved the speedy weather. The sisters watched it together, sucking at ice cubes, lying on their bellies with their four legs waving in the air. Time-travelling in their lounge room with the aid of the camera's shrewd lie.

*

Mr Sakamoto was waiting in drizzling rain outside the cinema. His felt hat bore a fringe of raindrops along the rim. He had already bought the tickets. When he saw Alice approach, he looked concerned.

'What have you done to yourself?' he asked, his tone alarmed.

And Alice realised that all afternoon she had worn the bloody scarf, strident as a blazon, decorating her chest as if she were the survivor, the one who was walking wounded, as if she had been kicked with steel boots in the pit of the Métro. Alice unwound the scarf with some embarrassment and stuffed it into her shoulder bag.

'Someone was hurt,' she said cryptically. 'Don't worry; it's not my blood.'

And although she could tell Mr Sakamoto wanted to know more, Alice fell silent.

What happens in a movie theatre? There is a transitional phase between the real and the screen, in which one views ironically, with everyday scepticism. Then at some point one falls headlong into the screen – there is an occult coalescence, a portal, a transfer, where the evidence of the senses is suddenly hijacked into fakery and exaggeration. It is a kind of release of self, a benign absorption. *Ninotchka* told the story of a Bolshevik apparatchik (Greta Garbo), who came to Paris in the thirties to supervise a delegation of three idiots, abroad with the task of selling jewels confiscated from White Russians. It was farcical and lighthearted, with a witty script. Ninotchka began as an ideologue, but was converted through love to enjoy the decadence of the capitalist West, which she nevertheless insisted was crumbling into destruction. Paris was a city of lavish attractions and overflowing desire. At the nadir of her ideological betrayal, Ninotchka wore a ridiculous hat, which she had bought as a guilty secret. This, and learning to laugh, were the symbols of her defection.

All through the movie Alice could hear Mr Sakamoto's response. He snorted, chuckled, exclaimed, laughed outright. Around them other cinema patrons also laughed; in the extraterrestrial light of the black-and-white movie they looked glazed with pleasure, heightened and abstracted into filmy emotions. Alice could see the rumbling of their shoulders and their backward jerks of amusement. It was something childish; it was something profoundly of the body. Encouraged by this disinhibition, Alice began also to laugh, and found that the spirit of sadness she had carried all afternoon, the taint of the Métro, and the woman who had stained her, gradually dissipated. When they swept outside, into the cold street, she felt she had been cleansed by comedy.

Mr Sakamoto was still cheerfully smiling. 'Wasn't it wonderful?' he exclaimed. 'I love the scene where Ninotchka finally laughs.'

Over drinks in a small bar Alice told Mr Sakamoto of the incident in the Métro, of the journey to the bookshop. She told him about the woman with the tattooed arm. Then she said that although she was studying modernity, she had bought a novel by Henry James.

'So what is the problem?' he asked. 'You are large enough to contain contradictions. We are all large enough – are we not? – to contain contradictions.'

Mr Sakamoto had first seen *Ninotchka* when he was eight years old. He had understood nothing of the plot – although his sisters had tried to explain Bolshevism and the idiotic delegation – but was seduced by Greta Garbo's luminous white face ('as though she wore Japanese rice powder') and the perceptibly sexual cadence of her laugh.

'It was a deep laugh,' he said, 'not a meretricious tinkle, such as passes for female laughter in movies today . . .'

Afterwards he and his sisters had gone to a teahouse where they all practised imitating Greta Garbo's laugh. Sachiko was the best. She threw back her head and let loose a thunderous sound. Accidentally she knocked over a cup of green tea, and then laughed again, with the others joining in. The owner of the teahouse thought they were misbehaved: three children laughing at nothing, talking in foreign languages and playing the fool.

Mr Sakamoto smiled knowingly. 'Not that I've seen many contemporary movies,' he added.

That night, Alice lay in bed, insomniac, thinking of Garbo's face, thinking of cinema. Mr Sakamoto was right; she would have to include it. Something in his story about the children practising a film-star laugh had impressed and moved her. She saw the three of them in a sepia light, hunched together in conspiratorial play, emboldened and united by movie-life mimicry. The screen carried fantasies writ large, but also bestowed games, gestural repertoires and collective stories; bestowed, moreover, a few images that stayed a lifetime, as if produced in intaglio. It was not mere absorption, but some kind of transaction. Not loss of self, but some fictive complication. Alice had heard the stuttering turn of the film strip, gearing up into expanded vision, had seen the cone of dusty light gleaming in the darkness, then the roaring big-headed

lion, the list of august names, before the swiftly seamless –
voilà! – conveyance-to-elsewhere. She had felt Mr Sakamoto
settle and relax beside her and begin to chuckle at the very
first scene. Aerospace light flashed down upon them. They
were rocketed off at twenty-four frames per second.

*

Let me tell you, *wrote Mr Sakamoto*, about the
felicitously named Lumière brothers, Auguste and Louis,
fine fellows with black eyes and handlebar moustaches,
who invented, as we all know, the *cinématographe* – the
cinema – in 1895. Their story begins with Antoine, their
father, a hale and hearty fellow, a singer and artist, who
married at nineteen, and had an energetic appreciation
of all things new. He set himself up as a painter of
portraits, then as a portrait photographer, in Lyon,
France. His son Louis, by the time he was eighteen,
had established a factory in the city for producing
photographic glass plates. This was an immensely
successful business, employing three hundred people
and producing fifteen million plates a year, for sale all
over Europe.

In 1894 Antoine was invited to Paris to see a
demonstration of Thomas Edison's kinetoscope
machine. This was a kind of large wooden box, with a
viewing peephole at the top, by which one person at a
time, leaning forward, peering from above, could see
tapes of film composed at Mr Edison's studios. Antoine
stood above the box, removed his top hat, and looked
deep into its fancy chute of darkness. He saw there a
slim woman dancing seductively with veils trailing
from her arms. '*Mon dieu!*' Antoine hurried back to
Lyon, excited by animated images, and charged his sons

with the task of devising a means by which these films could be projected for an audience, like magic lantern shows. One year later, they had it: the *cinématographe*, a box on a tripod. Hand-cranked, it both recorded and then projected images into the world. With an ingenious sprocket, a claw for moving film, they had found a device to put framed pictures into motion.

It would not be unkind to say that the brothers Auguste and Louis lacked the artistic flair of their excitable father. At the world's first screening, in the Grand Café in Paris, they showed images of their employees leaving the factory and a train arriving at a station, and would continue to film commonplace and even trite occurrences for years to come. They had no notion of story, or of special effect. Each film strip was fifty seconds of ordinary looking. A fixed camera position. Copycat filming. In 1895, however, it caused a sensation. How the café patrons ducked and cried out when the train moved towards them! How they exclaimed with relief and laughed when it stopped on the screen! This small sequence had about it the glow of inauguration. The train pulls up, heaves, pauses before us, and passengers begin in jerky fast motion to disembark. There are women in mutton-chop sleeves and puffy dresses of tulle, and men with hats and waistcoats, almost trotting along. A woman in a hat of extravagant size seizes a girl by the hand and charges towards the camera. One passenger, only one, seems to notice the camera on the platform. He is a sprightly young lad, perhaps only nineteen or twenty. He pauses, scrutinises, bends for a curious moment to examine this unknown box. He edges away, unsure. He is the first man in history screened thus, made self-conscious, selected from the crowd by the return of his gaze. It is a riveting moment. We in the audience love him. We make him the historical vehicle for all that phantasmically follows.

*

From the window of her studio, Alice watched the students at their break. They all seemed to be aged between fourteen and seventeen, and were therefore at the vulnerable, gawky age of indistinct character, vague ambition and obligatory fights with parents. As time passed, she began to see them individually, and felt a kind of long-distance affection for a few she habitually observed. There was a boy – she called him Leo – who was always alone. He had light brown hair and a thin angular face, and he always stood apart, moving in small, autistic jerks to the sound of his clamped-on headphones. Music was either his singular passion, or the device by which he excluded himself from others (or recognised *their* exclusion) in a socially plausible way. Leo always wore the same clothes – a sweater with a hood, tattered jeans – and did not smoke. His narrow body was restless, driven by music only he could hear, pounding directly into his eardrums. There was something pitiable about him, something lost.

Alice also liked to observe 'the lovers', whom she called Gisele and Sylvain. They spent much of each break together, against the wall, embracing and kissing. Their kisses had an intense prolongation and a gorgeous succulence. When they disengaged, they stood close together, the planes of their bodies still touching, their arms still entwined. The other students seemed to respect the relationship and did not interrupt or intrude. Sometimes Alice saw Sylvain joking with the others – his possession of Gisele gave him a certain swagger – but mostly they were interlocked, alone in their own way as Leo, listening to his music.

Among the students there was also a conspicuous girl. She

87

was popular, and laughed loudly, in a way Mr Sakamoto would like. She wore what appeared to be layers of rags and had spiky purple hair. Her confidence was wonderful to behold. 'Arlette' seemed to attend school only infrequently, but when she did, she was highly visible, attracting others, making noise, slipping between groups, linking them with her own intentions. The students around her talked on mobile phones and sent text messages to each other. They were all in a circuit of voices and signs; they were their own community.

Alice thought about her students, back at the university in Australia. They would now be attending lectures and writing essays. Feigning interest, nodding, pretending to have read the text. She did not miss her teaching. What she missed was contact with youth, with those who practised an assertion in the world that they took to be theirs, who saw their cities as intelligible territory, written for them, replete, awaiting, charged with intensities, who lived knitted in uttermost, secretive ways.

When Mr Sakamoto had said goodbye after the movie he had held up his hand to the side of his face, with the fingers curled and the thumb extended, making the shape of a telephone.

'I'll call you,' he'd said as Alice began moving away.

'I don't have a phone,' she had replied with a grin. 'I'll call *you*. Tomorrow. At the hotel.'

It was only later that she realised she had never seen anyone of Mr Sakamoto's age make the telephonic shorthand gesture. It was an action only young people performed. It was a code of twenty-something stockbrokers and fashion designers. Of cool baristas and film students and girls-who-wanted-to-be-models. Mr Sakamoto belonged to times other than his own; the habits of his body displayed forms of appropriated youthfulness. Perhaps the telephone had unfixed him, made him radically contemporary.

★

'Tell me exactly how Bell's telephone worked.'

'Well,' said Mr Sakamoto, 'there is first of all the medieval principle of rays in emanation . . .'

'Seriously,' she insisted.

'Two things, that's all. Number one: electromagnetism. Electric currents generate a magnetic field around themselves. The stronger the current, the stronger the field. You send a current through a coil of wire, and the iron core of the coil is magnetised. The current can be varied in strength and the electromagnet can vibrate a flexible iron diaphragm and create a sound, any sound, even a human voice. Number two: induction. Induction is about using sound itself to vary the current. Induction means that a changing magnetic field generates currents in the circuit. So when the sound of a voice vibrates, the changes in the magnetic field induce a similarly varying current.'

'I think I prefer the principle of rays in emanation.'

'Yes,' admitted Mr Sakamoto. 'Voice; it's really all about voice. It's about ripples in the air, patterns of ripples, as in a Japanese raked garden. Do you know the raked garden? Have you seen them in photographs?'

Alice nodded.

'The raked garden always looks to me like an image of sound waves. Gardens, ocean, the beauty of energy transmission. *Tele-phone*: sound at a distance.'

They were walking slowly together by the river. The sun was shining and traces of early spring blossom, like flakes of brown tissue, hung in the moderate wind. There were dogs and pigeons; there were babies in strollers. Roller skaters swept along the footpaths, weaving between pedestrians with imperious confidence. The streets were lively, bright.

Mr Sakamoto halted. 'There,' he said, 'that's the third one I've seen.' He pointed to the word 'nuance' in white paint, in a neat cursive hand, at the foot of a wall. 'Superior graffito, don't you think?'

They stood looking together, each in meditation.

'Do you know,' asked Alice, 'about Mr Eternity?'

All the way to the bistro – which Mr Sakamoto had insisted on revisiting, in order, he said, to comprehend the battle between the waiters – Alice told him the story.

There was once in Sydney, Australia, a man called Arthur Stace. Born in 1884, he was of a miserable background; his mother, father and siblings were all alcoholics. He grew up in poverty. At twelve he was made a ward of the state; he got his first job at fourteen, working in a coal mine, and by fifteen found himself in gaol. In his twenties he engaged in various criminal activities and then in the First World War he served in France, returning physically and spiritually broken. He was suffering shell shock and the effects of mustard gas, and was also partially blinded in one eye. Arthur sank further and further into a life of dereliction and alcoholism, buying methylated spirits, 'white lady', at sixpence a bottle. Some time in 1930 he visited a Baptist food handout centre, and heard a fire-and-brimstone preacher give a remarkable sermon. The preacher stated he would like to shout the word 'ETERNITY' in every street in Sydney. This was Arthur Stace's conversion experience. He was overcome with a need to write the word 'eternity', in chalk or crayon, on the pavements of Sydney. For thirty-seven years – rising at 5 a.m., praying, then following God's directions to a particular site – he inscribed the word almost half a million times. He wrote in a copperplate hand, with a flourish on the 'E' and an extended tail on the 'Y', which served to underline the whole word. Urban myths abounded about Mr Eternity, but he was unmasked in the fifties and with great shyness and humility accepted the identity and confessed his inscriptions. He died, aged eighty-three, in 1967, having gifted to the city these frail repetitions, this heavenly mania, this lovely obsession.

'It's a true story,' Alice added emphatically.

Mr Sakamoto stopped. 'It's a wonderful story. 'Nuance' and 'eternity': these are the two dimensions of *haiku*. I shall give you a book, one of my favourites. In translation, of course.'

They had halted at a florist shop, before a line of cyclamen. The pink and purple flowers had a stunning vivacity. Alice could smell the scent of turned soil, cross-hatched with small implements.

'Wait here,' she said.

Mr Sakamoto waited as Alice bought a pot of bright flowers, wrapped in tissue paper. When she emerged from the florists she handed the purchase to her friend. He looked surprised. He bowed and appeared abashed.

'No one has ever bought me flowers before,' he said shyly.

In the bistro they discussed the time of modernity as Mr Sakamoto observed the waiters. He did not accept, he said, that all was despotic acceleration and unholy speed. The hunger for nuance and eternity infiltrated the lives of everyone, even the speediest executive. It was this that caused a businessman to pause, in dim light, and listen in the shadows to his sleeping child breathing.

'You're romanticising,' Alice accused him. 'He's neglected

his children and is just checking to see what they look like.'

'Perhaps,' he said. 'But perhaps he wants, if only for a moment, to stand in the time of a small child's breath. The time of softest intuitions.'

The soup arrived. *Potage du jour* was a thick potato. The waiter snarled as he deposited the plates.

'Did you know,' Mr Sakamoto went on, 'that Alexander Graham Bell, inventor of the telephone, liked to drink his soup through glass tubes and straws of various circumferences? It infuriated his wife.'

With this statement he plunged in his spoon and began heartily to eat. The pot of cyclamen rested on the table between them, the vivid effusion of what Alice had not been able to say.

7

Let me tell you, *wrote Mr Sakamoto*, about Alexander
Graham Bell.

I have spent almost eight years now, contemplating
this splendid fellow, composing his story, tracking
with biographical monomania all the flaunted public
events and hidden private emotions, the chronology,
the secrets, the lies, the loves, the disasters, the eventual, astonishing fame. It is folly, my project. The
more facts one accumulates, the more one doubts.
And the more one adores the subject, the more he
seems capricious, external, gone. I was attracted to
Bell because he invented the telephone, and it was an
invention borne not purely of technical know-how
and electromechanical challenge, but because, above
all, he loved the human voice. The voice, above all.
He was a teacher of voice, as were his father and
grandfather before him. The telephone is the blessing
and completion of speech. It drags from nowhere and
everywhere utterances great and small; it secures
connections; it knits emotions. It conveys the tiniest
sigh – the wind of one single person, yearning, alone
– to the ear of a lover, waiting, in another country. I
see you now, dear Alice, raising your eyebrow, but my

wish is to persuade you that the telephone is in the end munificent. I write not of ringing the plumber, or making a dental appointment, but the realm of exclamation, confession, poetry, love. Everyone has experienced this: a moment in conversation that equals to standing naked before strangers and feeling undiminished and wholly alive.

Alexander's grandfather, also Alexander Bell, began as an actor in Scotland, but left the stage to teach elocution and correct stammering in children. His wife had a scandalous affair with the rector of Dundee, so he divorced her and moved to London with his small son, Alexander (my Alexander's father). There he published *The Practical Elocutionist* and a book on stammering, and met with a small degree of fame as a master of the tongue. Indeed, odd as it sounds, among his publications is 'The Tongue', 1232 lines of blank verse proclaiming the beauty of elocution. The next Alexander followed his father into the business of speech, and set himself up as a 'Professor of Elocution' and a public performer of the works of Charles Dickens. (He was reputed to read Dickens better than the author himself.) He also published a book, *The Standard Elocutionist*. More importantly, he fell in love with Eliza Symonds, a painter of miniatures, a woman ten years older than himself and almost entirely deaf, though she could detect sound very faintly with the assistance of a speaking tube. This loving couple settled in Edinburgh, and Eliza bore three sons, Melville (Melly), Alexander (Alec, my Alexander Bell, in 1847) and Edward (Ted).

Of all the childhood stories I have encountered, there are three, in particular, I wish to share with you.

Alec experienced the usual trials and tribulations —
a nasty bout, for example, of scarlet fever, which kept
him alone in an isolated and darkened room — but one
event of distress strikes me as predictive and symbolic.
On a family excursion to Ferny Hill, Alec became lost
in a wheat field. He lay down, out of fear, and all he
saw was the iron sky and the bars of millions of
trembling wheat stalks. He was a small frightened
boy, separated from his family, and trapped in a sour-
smelling wheat field with the sky pressing down. Then
Alec heard his father's voice calling his name: 'Alec!
Alec!' and by tracking the voice he was returned and
saw before him his father, who now appeared gigantic,
standing with open arms and moist bleary eyes. The
name that connected them in generations was also an
occasion of rescuing sound, and Alec learned then, in
this space of almost biblical resonance, that speech and
hearing were also his vocation.

The second story concerns his mother, Eliza.
Although as an adult he would not budge from
staunch agnosticism, Alec was a devout believer as a
child and attended church each Sunday with his
mother and brothers. Eliza could not hear the
minister, so the three brothers took turns at the
speaking tube, in order that she might follow the
service. Alec discovered that he could bypass the
tube altogether and communicate with his mother by
talking in a very low voice, with his lips positioned
close, almost touching, at her forehead. In this
intimate way he conveyed divine service; at a lover's
proximity he retold the sermon and directed her to
biblical passages and the order of hymns. He had seen
his mother play the piano by placing the mouthpiece

95

of her speaking tube directly on the sounding board, and knew that there existed a near realm of sympathetic vibration. Eliza played duets with her husband on the flute, while Ted, the most musically gifted of the sons, sang in accompaniment. And since his father had created an alphabet of 'Visible Speech', symbols of a universal representation of sound in almost every language, Alec knew that the tissue that separated visibility and invisibility, sound and silence, was unusually permeable. As he practised Urdu and Arabic and a dozen European languages, he knew too that the mystery of speech is as much metaphysical as physical – it had to do with design, as well as will, with the heart, as well as the larynx. With his lips almost touching his mother's head, Alec understood that some forms of communication are essentially loving, and carry within them esteem, closeness, solicitation.

The third story I must tell you is about Alec and his dog, a stray Skye terrier that turned up one day at their house, wagging his tail and pleading implicitly, as dogs always do, for immediate friendship. The boys named it Trouve. Alec embarked on a lunatic programme to teach Trouve to speak. Over weeks he trained the dog to growl on cue and to produce a particular sequence of sounds: 'ow, ah, ooh, ga, ma, ma', which he claimed resembled – and in fact it did – 'How are you grandmama?' The family was enchanted. Poor Trouve was doomed to repeat his trick, but was also, as dogs are, patiently compliant. With his brother Melly, Alec went on to try to construct an actual speaking machine using – since Melly, also a speech man, nevertheless fancied himself an anatomist – the fleshy larynx extracted from a dead cat. It was a grisly failure. So Alec contented himself with his dog's obliging simulation.

I love the child Alexander, but it is his losses, I think, that most move and engage me. When he was twenty years old his younger brother, Ted, by then eighteen, strikingly handsome, and well over six feet tall, died of tuberculosis. Alec and Melly also suffered severe bouts of illness, and their parents grew fearful and overprotective. Three years later Melly, to whom Alec was closest, also died of the disease. The brothers had made a pact that whomever died first, the other would try, by all means possible, to establish spirit communication. Alec attended seance after seance, but Melly did not speak. He watched his parents weep together, holding their hands in a knot. They embraced and leaned compassionately in each other's direction, expressing in tears the solidarity of grief. But Alec felt alone, and guilty, and saved for no purpose. He experienced periods of migraine and began working on experiments late at night: for the rest of his life, he went to bed at 4 a.m. We could say, perhaps, that darkness entered him. Grief made more sense in the middle of the night, when he could imagine, for small periods, that he was deaf like his mother, or that he had entered the antechamber of the dead – this still, deep dark, this brotherless otherworld. In the daytime Alec attended to Melly's speech clients, concentrating on one he especially liked, a young Australian man with the dual afflictions of bad skin and an embarrassing lisp.

At length Alec left Trouve and his parents behind and moved to America to become a teacher of speech to the deaf. He worked in Boston, at a school for thirty deaf boys and girls, and after that, at the age of twenty-four, began lecturing and accepting small numbers of private students. He took up the Chair of Vocal Physiology and Elocution in the School of Oratory at Boston University, and in the meantime had fallen in love with one of his students – pretty Mabel Hubbard, a girl struck deaf in early childhood by an episode of scarlet fever. She was sixteen years old and incompetent at vowels. She was spirited and had the habit of chewing on her curls. Her manner was lively, her pink smile was a charm. Alec was smitten. After two long years of persuasion, her parents agreed to a betrothal on Mabel's eighteenth birthday. Mabel announced that she was not in love with Alexander Bell, but neither did she dislike him. For Alec, this was enough.

He had already taken out his patent for the electric speech device. After a series of experiments, which included the electrical stimulation of a dead man's ear, the success he had in 1875 would prove to be legendary. Recorded for posterity are his ordinary words to his friend, 'Mr Watson come here; I want to see you' and the fact that Watson, beyond earshot, then repeated the words. They had filtered to him, precisely, through this gadget that by means invisible wed faraway voices. On the strength of his invention Bell at last married, and returned to Scotland. There he began to transform; he began to consume. He ate the foods of his childhood – porridge, eggs, slabs of thick bread – in mountainous quantities. Perhaps the memory of his skeletal brothers pursued and haunted him; perhaps he was trying to take into his body whatever it was he had lost. In any case, Alec ate and ate until he changed shape entirely, and became a barrel of a man, someone others found imposing. Mabel was critical of her husband's expanding girth, but to no avail. And then her body also expanded: in time she give birth to two daughters, Elsie May and Marion.

What had he created? Some technologies are coercive, some seductive. The telephone lassoed floating desires and pulled them in: it offered the satisfactions of tacit connection, indulgent expression and the fantasy of a limitless, out-reaching voice. Beyond its practical applications, it offered subtler pleasures. The eroticism of entering, weightless and irresponsible, someone else's bedroom in the middle of the night. The exchange of the complaints and pleasures that are the texture of the everyday. The delight of a small child's halting communication, full of serious silences and bursts of random information. Whispered endearments and outright invitations. Deals. Agreements. Negotiations. Extended monologues. Cross-planetary greetings. Affectionate hellos.

Bodies fell away and speakers entered voice-time. The space between them squeezed open and shut like an accordion. Mere dialling was a thrill. The sound of ringing far off, and the conjuring-up of a distant, unseen room. The efficient stiff click as the receiver was lifted. The initial enquiry. 'Yes?' The relaxation into dialogue. The visionless, undivided exchange. It was not a new alienation, but a new return, a creation of selves reconnected by breathing words into a black bulb of moulded plastic.

At its inception Alexander Bell was engaged in

ludicrous acts of publicity. The telephone was demonstrated in the depths of a Newcastle coal mine, then beneath the Thames, between quizzical divers. A private demonstration was arranged for Queen Victoria, for which – since ordinary talk was considered unroyal – a woman was hired to sing 'Kathleen Mavourneen' into the mouthpiece. She did so superbly. Queen Victoria was amused. Alec posed smiling in numerous photographs with august politicians. His fat Spanish-looking face, with its impressive fanned beard, adorned the covers of magazines and the flimsy pages of newspapers. The Bell family subsequently moved back to America. They became millionaires, bought a huge estate, and began a series of worldwide journeys that betrayed the inner restlessness of Alec's spirit. He continued relentlessly to invent, and to work late into the nights, so that he maintained against the insistent clamorousness of fame his alternative world of dark and silence.

Two other significant losses burdened Alexander Bell. In 1881, a son, Edward, was born, but died in infancy, unable to fill his tiny lungs with life. For his son Bell invented a 'vacuum jacket', designed to create artificial respiration. It was an airtight iron cylinder, fitted up to the neck, which reduced air pressure around the body and so forced air in through the mouth – an anticipation of the iron-lung device. But little Edward's life was not to be saved; the vacuum jacket was a fitted coffin. Alec saw his son encased in his failure. As a distraction from grief, Alec and Mabel once again resumed travelling; they took their young daughters on a swift trip to Paris. There, and in secret, Alec commissioned a French artist to paint a portrait of his dead son (after a sketch made at home) resting, as though asleep, in his satin-lined casket. He showed no one this painting, but kept it to himself, like guilt. And when he mourned, he gazed upon it to increase his mournfulness to its full measure of profundity.

Two years later, the Bells lost their second son, Robert, also in infancy. It was a devastating repetition. Alec grieved for his lost sons all his life. He was not reconciled and he did not believe in God's will. He believed in the invention of electrical devices to alleviate the suffering of humanity.

Of his later career as the world-famous inventor of the telephone, Alec was ambivalent. He consistently cited his occupation as 'teacher of voice to the deaf' and his most complex relationship was with the blind-deaf woman Helen Keller, in a silent film of whose remarkable life he later made a cameo appearance, starring as himself. In her company, Alec sought again what rested beyond speech, what meanings became pronounced in detachment, what value might be given to enclosed states of being. Sometimes, late at night, he felt a kinship with Helen Keller beyond any reason. He stared at the black night sky and imagined himself absorbed; he listened to the silence behind the sigh of the wind, and the creaking of floorboards and all the minute unseeable night-time things that existed in murmurs and ticks and barely audible scamperings. Helen had touched his hands with articulate signs and expressed the spiritual rewards of her unchosen isolation. Alec felt that he understood. That there was a sympathy between them. An unremarked vibration. And as the night passed over his head, like the drawing of a heavy cloak that disguised his human shape, he almost fancied he heard the voices of Melly and Ted, and the strained feeble breathing of his dying sons, soft and close and enticing as death.

Worldly considerations at length reclaimed Alexander Graham Bell. He experimented with the breeding of sheep and the mechanisms of flight; he investigated underwater foghorns and radiophonic possibilities. When, in 1881, the President, James Garfield, was shot in the back as he walked through the Washington railway station, Alec arrived at the White House with a metal detector of his own devising, in order to locate the hidden bullet. This was another of his failures, and the President, lying on a mattress reinforced by many coiled metal springs, died, aged forty-nine, with the missile undetected and still lodged fatally in his body.

There were court cases, money matters, business dealings, grandchildren, more and more money. Alexander Bell moved into ultra-celebrity. When he died at seventy-five, in 1922, he had read the *Encyclopædia Britannica* from end to end, had invented dozens of contraptions beside the telephone, and was a man still privately wedded to hush, to dark, to sign, to grief. His overlarge body, swollen with dense Scottish food, was deposited by his weeping family and everywhere eulogised. Wee images of his face appeared on postage stamps across the world. No one could quite remember the sound of his voice.

8

The more Alice and Mr Sakamoto met, the more they liked each other. Their initial recognition of affinity, built with lopsided speculation in a brief encounter on the train, had been confirmed and extended in conversations and shared city walks. He was a man not just enraptured by telephones and Alexander Graham Bell, but given over to vigilant apprehension of the world made both destructible and glorious by its many technologies. He remembered the bomb, but he also delighted in gadgetry. He was respectful of vast machinery, but pondered the mechanism of a corkscrew and the intricacy of old clocks. When they sat in parks he noticed the tiniest things: the nervous vectors of a single sparrow, the mottled colours and arrangements of fallen leaves, the rainy tints in the afternoon sky. This was a capacity, he said, that had come from the practice of *haiku*, which he thoroughly recommended to everyone he met. There was a fabric of knowing, he claimed, beyond vision, beyond hearing. Just as dogs practise an apparently subsonic intelligence, or birds know by inner geometry their flight paths and havens, so there are latent forms of life everywhere and secret understandings. Richer than silicon, he said. Hyperlinked without end.

Mr Sakamoto's interest in technology, Alice discovered, was bound principally with characters and stories. He spent hours reading biographies, or searched on the internet, finding the details of inventors' lives and filling in gaps with the stuff of his own preoccupations. When he offered to send Alice occasional biographical notes, she agreed. It seemed a pleasant way to extend their friendship. By this means she became the recipient of Mr Sakamoto's meditations on inventors, tales charming and loopy, informative and daft.

The balance between them, a lighthearted, almost comic, equipoise of anecdote and observation, shifted when Mr Sakamoto listened to Alice's distress. He had earlier listened with knowing quiet as she told him of the violence in the Métro, and the old woman who displayed her blue tattoo; but an incident concerning Leo led to a phone call in the night and her voice sent towards him with desperate force. Mr Sakamoto heard Alice's soft-speaking voice strain against weeping. He heard her tear apart. He felt for her almost exactly as he felt for his daughters: a great and virtuous love, a wish above all to give solace.

It began when Alice returned one evening from the library, weighted with her papers and ideas, caught in the distractions of her project. When she turned the corner into her street she thought, for an absurd moment, that someone was making a movie. There were lights, roped off areas, police in natty uniforms and shiny boots holding back a small curious crowd. Voices were interested, engaged. But as she pushed forward she realised it was something else, it was something terrible. She explained to the police officer standing nearest that the door of her apartment building was in the cordoned-off area, and asked if she might pass. It was only then, having ducked under the light-reflecting tape and entered the site of emergency, that she saw him. The boy she had called Leo, the boy she had watched day after day, rocking to his own music, wired for personal sound, tuned in, autonomous, lay dead in the doorway opposite, his head propped, as though arranged, so that he appeared to be looking her way. Leo's young face was pulpy and crudely disfigured. A man kneeled beside him, making notes.

'Leo,' Alice exclaimed, with a weak involuntary shout.

Everyone seemed to turn in her direction.

'You know this boy?' someone asked.

'Yes. No.' She corrected herself.

'Leo who? What is his surname?'

Alice was obliged to reveal that she did not know the boy, that she had never met him, or talked to him, or even nodded as he passed by, that 'Leo' was a kind of fantasy connection. The policeman looked irritated. Alice added that he attended the school at the end of the street. The policeman wrote this down. He asked Alice if she had seen anyone suspicious in the street, anyone talking to 'Leo'. Anyone harassing him. Any drugs. Any fights. Any prostitution. Alice knew nothing.

'I know nothing,' she heard herself blandly pronounce. '*Je sais rien.*'

Her throat was dry and her hands were trembling. Over the policeman's shoulder she could see the still uncovered boy, his face battered and black-looking, the nose clearly broken. The hood of his parka was askew, exposing a gash along his cheek. One eye was half open. The lights of the investigation were startlingly bright. Alice saw her own street as she had never seen it before. Brutality accentuated it, made it sharp and irrefutable. There was a stain of piss on the wall, not far from the body. Crumpled paper in the gutter. A shredded and illegible poster, peeling like human skin. Alice heard a cough, an impatience; the policeman found this foreigner wearisome.

'Go inside,' he said. 'Now.'

Alice fumbled for her keys and obediently entered her building. She felt herself stagger up the uneven stairs to her studio, full of a weight in her chest that was like a brick, like a sob, like a dead thing lodged inside. She sat in the dark, at the window, watching all that happened below. For a long time the men in the street just mingled and talked. Then Alice saw Leo's body sealed in a black vinyl bag, lifted into a van and taken away. The reflecting tape was dismantled, wound on a spool like a film. The cars began to withdraw. She saw the last two policemen having a quiet cigarette. They joked about something: there was a moment of cruel laughter. When finally they departed, Alice ran downstairs, outside, and acting purely on instinct, skidded into the telephone booth on the corner and rang Mr Sakamoto at his hotel. He asked her to wait while he turned off the television in his room, and then he listened.

Alice spoke to Mr Sakamoto of the battered face. She spoke of the boy who was named and not named Leo, the boy she had known and not known, who was treated like garbage, left dumped in the street, destroyed, made ugly. She spoke of the sorrowfulness of the night and the sound that was never the river. She spoke of the way the policemen's lights made everything inhuman, and the waste of it, and the pity, and the fierce anonymity. She told him of the joke she could not hear, and the implicit disrespect. The forms of negation that inhere in a single flicked butt, or a tone of voice, or a flung paper cup, consigned to litter.

Alice was aware of making awkward gestures in the glass box of the telephone booth. She was aware too that she talked quickly and probably made no sense at all. But still she spoke, and still she imparted to the ear of gentle Mr Sakamoto her vision of the thin boy's face, robbed of life, and the central shadow in the street that was his fallen body, and the police with their stubborn persistence, simply hanging around. How undramatic they were. They had acted as if the world was orderly and sound. As if it were an everyday occurrence, this propped body, this offence.

At some point in her monologue, Alice became self-conscious.

'Forgive me,' she said, 'I don't know why I'm telling you all this. Bothering you in the middle of the night.'

But Mr Sakamoto pacified and reassured her.

'Do you want company?' he asked. 'Do you want me to come over? Or I could get you a room here. We could drink coffee together.'

But Alice said no. She was suddenly nervous of the intimacy of spoken words. The spilled emotion. Her unguarded display. They arranged to meet the next day at their usual bistro.

When she thought about it afterwards, she was surprised at her lack of restraint and uncharacteristic will to disclosure. It had been a summoning of despair into language, and its release through the telephone. All that black wind that had rushed to occupy her, all that night-time distortion and sense of despoliation, she had converted into words and sentences for Mr Sakamoto, just as he did, in another scale, in an entirely other scale, for his Uncle Tadeo. It was an experience of the strange tenderness of hyperbolic moments. The emptying joy.

Over their lunch Alice resumed her clumsy apology.

'I can't believe how I went on and on last night. About the joke. About the river. I didn't know what I was saying.'

'It's OK. Really. Everyone needs inside them an ocean or a river.'

Alice had heard him but wasn't sure how to respond.

'It was an overreaction,' she continued. 'I didn't even know him.'

'Not at all,' responded Mr Sakamoto. 'The death of the young is unacceptable. We should feel appalled and insulted. We should howl and complain. There is no overreaction to witnessed death.'

He looked out the window and seemed to have no appetite. He had a beautiful face, creased and burnished with sadness. His hair was silver, neat. He wore an impeccable dark grey suit and a red silk tie, patterned with chevrons. He might have been a Tokyo banker. Alice watched Mr Sakamoto push food around his plate. They left their meal half eaten, and walked by the Seine, in the wind-blown afternoon, companionable, now, in what was implicitly understood but could not be uttered, in what blew away, torn to shreds, in the wake of any calamity.

*

A woman inventor? Let me tell you about my favourite, Hedy Lamarr. Born Hedwig Eva Marie Kiesler, in Vienna, in 1913, she became a screen goddess of almost incomparable allure. In the silver economy, only Garbo rivalled her; in the field of enlarged pearly faces, fake eyelashes and suppliant poses, of swooning eroticism and deeply serious kisses, she was up there in the pantheon, genuinely adorable. Something in the filming of these women made them appear perpetually yielding. Their faces blurred with desire. They were languid, available. Lit from above, sumptuously, against a mound of silk pillows. When, as a young man, I saw her with Victor Mature in *Samson and Delilah*, I almost exploded with lust. Against Mature's chunky body she flung her scarcely clad self; her hair was wild and astray, her intentions profane. I thought she was magnificent. In real life she married and divorced six times. She was a regular attractor.

Hedy Lamarr's status as an inventor is less well known. Her first husband, Fritz Mandl, was a wealthy munitions dealer who sided with the Nazis, and Hedy left him and fled to London – but not before she had learned something of arms design and proposed the invention of a radio-controlled torpedo. When Hedy ended up in America, signed by Louis Mayer with MGM, she decided to aid the allied war effort by reviving her torpedo ideas. The problem, as she saw it, was their interception. With the help of a composer, George Antheil, who knew something of frequencies, she devised a plan to use frequency hopping to make it impossible to track and intercept torpedoes. Their joint patent application was hugely successful, and George duly gave credit to the actress who originated the idea.

It is the quality of anomaly that makes Hedy Lamarr's case so important. No other screen goddess bothered herself with torpedoes, with the calculation of jamming radio signals and the logistics of random transmission. We must picture her on the set of *Tortilla Flat*, perhaps, or the dreadful *Algiers*, or the even worse *White Cargo*, gazing into the camera and imagining explosions. As she spoke her corny lines, or kissed her beefcake heroes, she thought – possibly with a kind of amoral abstraction – of sinking ships and sailors struggling to stay afloat in the ocean, of desperate men grasping at splintered wreckage, of men flailing and drowning, men with contorted faces, frantic with fear.

*

Alice was missing television. After long days of reading and writing, she wanted the uncomplicated comfort of serial images. She wanted a sofa on which to recline, and before it a moulded luminous box, solid and commanding as a shrine. Like plastic bags and mobile phones, television was both a facile utility and a tacky satisfaction. The news she read in newspapers seemed less real without its animating images; the weather report less credible without comic-book clouds and suns tacked onto colourful national maps; and her narrative hunger, which was massive, was unassuaged. She wondered if the story of Leo's murder had been shown on television, if she would have been able to see his weeping mother, and his father, grim and brave and wearing a tilted shabby cap, just holding back the tears as he spoke of his loss. Perhaps there was a shot of his house, somewhere, and a younger brother or two, looking bewildered and estranged, peering with suspicion at the television crew, who nevertheless managed efficiently and brutally to intrude. Perhaps too, he had a pretty sister, almost his age and looking very like him, with the same thin pallid face and nervy manner, who announced to the camera that he was the best brother ever to have lived, and that he adored animals and video games and popular music.

Alice felt ashamed of herself for these prepackaged imaginings, and wondered if they were a consequence of her first impression that night, that she had stumbled upon a film set. The corruptibility of grief by routine image-making dismayed and upset her. Someone — perhaps friends from the school — had placed a posy in the doorway, where a telltale smear of blood was still apparent, but within hours the flowers had become ragged and a gust of wind sent white carnations rolling chaotically up the street. Alice thought at first that she might retrieve and replace them, but she did not. This event — the seeming authenticity of the laying of flowers by people who *actually* knew Leo, and their so-easy, so-quick ruination by wind — seemed to Alice symbolic of something irretrievably lost. She was unsure what to feel, or if feeling anything at all was not a kind of vague and luxurious self-indulgence to which, ultimately, she had no right. She didn't know him, after all. For all her shy voyeurism, she had never even said hello.

Cities generated these disorders of response between people, these misalignments of personal and public meaning. In large populations, crammed together, there were inevitably forms of disturbance and assaults to consciousness. Discharges of violence. Lives in collapse, knocking others as they fell. In photographs taken from the sky, cities resembled circuit boards. It was no surprise, really, that there were sparky misfirings, dangerous connections. Even traffic, Alice concluded, set up a kind of static in the air, let loose vibrations and uncontainable agitation. Freighted with more than they could absorb, with city intentions, citizens moved in designs of inexplicable purpose.

Even as she entertained these metaphors, Alice rejected them. The circuit was too predictable, too completely determinative. Yet she was reminded of her father, and of faraway childhood things, invisibly charged. His workman's hands clasping pliers, joining red and yellow wires with dextrous twisting and snapping and threading of copper. Objects flicked into being under electric lights. Simple incandescence. Simple shock. She had believed then in the fundamental electricity of things — of brains, of bodies, of whole communities.

By evening someone had replaced the flowers. Alice felt relieved. She gazed down upon them. More white carnations. Leo's makeshift memorial was still as fragile as ever. *Someone died here*. There was a long handwritten note pinned beneath the flowers. Imagining its tribute, Alice began to weep.

★

Shifts within friendships happen in imperceptible increments. There is distance, then assurance. Misconjecture, caution, gradual convergence. So much depends on the respect accorded to vulnerability.

Mr Sakamoto and Alice began talking more personally. They had enjoyed exchanging talks about inventions and modern objects, but now each ventured an occasional enquiry that signified the understanding between them, or was the token of a more relaxed and shared curiosity.

'What's the oddest thing you've seen on your travels,' Alice asked 'to do with misplaced technology? To do with things out of context.'

'That's easy,' Mr Sakamoto said. 'The Spanish astronaut.' Here he paused to elicit Alice's interest.

'Well?' she was forced to ask. She leaned forward and touched his hand.

Mr Sakamoto grinned. 'Only a year ago,' he began, 'I was visiting the city of Salamanca, in Spain. The cathedral, what they call the New Cathedral, which actually dates from the Renaissance, had been recently restored. The stonemasons added the carved image of an astronaut to the figures in a frieze around the door. There he was, suspended among ivy leaves and griffins and dogs and sheep, with his helmet and suit and gigantic boots. The oxygen line that attached him to his ship – not pictured, of course – lay across his belly like an umbilicus. His nose had already been knocked off, giving him a kinship with many of the ancient bishops and biblical figures elsewhere on the cathedral, earlier effaced . . .'

'At first,' Mr Sakamoto went on, 'I thought it a sacrilege, a kind of puerile mischief. But after a while it began to look more and more acceptable, and I thought it a comic touch – almost a theological point – about the inclusiveness of creation, about the sacredness of the joke, about the incorporation of every thing into the scheme of the cathedral . . . I'm not sure, really . . .

'There is also another dimension to this story. I had been to that very spot, to that very cathedral, years ago, when I was first married. I took my wife, Mie, on a European honeymoon. She had never been outside Japan, and I suppose I thought, rather proudly, that I would show her the world, I thought I would demonstrate my knowledge and be the one to offer new pleasures. I was anxious to make a positive impression, to make her love me. But Mie hated travelling. The trip was a disaster. She was disorientated and unhappy, and talked longingly of our home. Often she stayed in our hotel rooms, and left me to sightsee alone. She found the trains slow and inefficient, she hated the food. I wanted so much to bind us together and create a foundation of special memories to begin our marriage, but in the end had to concede I had misunderstood her. I felt ashamed. I had not even known her well enough to realise she would rather stay at home. In Salamanca I coaxed her to the cathedral: we stood before it – then unrestored – we were in a sunny plaza, it was a glorious spring day – and she burst into tears. Mie clutched at my arm and begged to be taken home. Spain was only the second country on our itinerary, but we returned to Japan within a few days. Last year, I revisited the towns and cities I had been to with Mie. I wanted to see them again, and also retrack those places we had stood together, if only in that tense and misguided way. I realise now how pompous I must have seemed, lecturing her on European culture, expecting her to like what I liked, to be deferential. I realised too how very mismatched we were, although we did come to love each other, after the girls arrived. Ours was a marriage, like many, which required each partner to suppress their truest identity, to become joint, to become a kind of functional unit.'

Mr Sakamoto fell silent. Perhaps he feared he had said too much. Then he smiled and asked: 'And you? What odd misplacement can you describe?'

'Nothing quite so interesting. About two years ago I went backpacking with my boyfriend, Stephen, in Indonesia. We were living fairly rough, trying to avoid the big centres, trying to set ourselves a challenge. On one of the islands there was an active volcano and you could hire a guide to take you walking to the summit and then down again. The walk took about ten hours and was almost impossibly strenuous. We left well before dawn, at about three in the morning, and the way was steep and treacherous, with loose stones and hazardous cliff-face manoeuvres, and towards the top there were sulphurous emissions that made us choke for air. We thought we were suffocating. Our eyes were streaming, our throats were sore, the earth beneath us was so hot that we could feel heat through our boots. Stephen told me afterwards that he was convinced that we would die there together, on that stinking slope, our faces burned to nothing by the ground where we fell. The Indonesian guide seemed unperturbed and hurried on, practically leaping up the volcano, while behind Stephen and I struggled to keep up, feeling foolish and exhausted. Our legs ached terribly and we were sunburned and frazzled. When at last we finally reached the summit, there before us was our nimble and nonchalant guide, smoking a clove cigarette, relaxing, looking pleased with himself, and a young German couple, who must have found their own way up the mountain. They were both resplendent – dressed in lime-coloured Lycra and reflective sunglasses. The man was speaking into a mobile phone. He spoke at the very top of his voice, and was presumably shouting to Germany of his latest excursion. Stephen and I looked at each other and laughed. We felt shabby and pathetic; we were so tired we weren't sure we could make the return journey, and there was a man, looking monumental, looking like an advertisement, with a mobile phone. The German couple were in fact polite and welcoming, and we all descended together, and shared a meal late in the evening . . .

'I know that the ubiquity of mobile phones is not a particularly arresting story, but the trek had been such a trial, we had felt we were at a point of extremity, that its appearance on the scene seemed more than usually absurd. In the village, below, there was not even electricity. And something about the way the man spoke – so loud and commanding, like a stockbroker, settling a deal – was truly shattering in the context of reaching the summit, finding oneself in the sky, standing over gas and molten earth at the point of physical collapse . . . We looked out at the landscape, barely able to stand – it was a vista of paddy fields and rolling hills and in the far distance, the ocean – and what we heard was shouted speech, sent up to a satellite.'

*

At their bistro it was a quiet time. Most of the diners had left, and afternoon satiety and lassitude was settling in. In restaurants this was marked by an orange quality to the light and an awareness of the inert and slightly smothering atmosphere of accumulated food scents. The last customers leaned back in their chairs, smoking and finishing wine. Mr Sakamoto excused himself, left the table and approached the taller and older of the two waiters, pausing before him to offer a bow.

Alice heard him speak in a low and confidential tone, his voice sounding rather like that of a counsellor. His French was accented, lucid and grammatically perfect.

The waiter tilted his head and listened, then a conversation began. Alice could not hear what they were saying, but saw the fierce interest of the other waiter, who pretended to polish glasses. At length the men shook hands and Mr Sakamoto turned and walked over to the younger waiter. Again, he bowed, then spoke politely and in a low respectful tone. Again, a conversation started, their heads inclined. At one point Alice heard what sounded like an exclamation of dismay, but mostly the talk was quiet and even in tone.

After ten minutes or so Mr Sakamoto returned to the table, and behind him the waiters moved together, and then embraced. It was an allegory of rapprochement, a simple performance, a silent victory.

'Lovers,' Mr Sakamoto said. 'I guessed it from the beginning. A ridiculous minor disagreement that had grown large and monstrous. They listen to me because they see me as an inscrutable foreigner, who doesn't understand the rules of social restraint. It enables me to say things. To intervene. So much can be achieved just by naming, and by asking the right questions. Do you love him? Is this worth it? They ask: what business is it of yours? None at all, I say. I am simply a stranger, passing through, who notices all this unnecessary unhappiness . . .'

Mr Sakamoto had already paid the bill, so he and Alice rose and left the bistro discreetly. They did not look back. It would have seemed intrusive, even triumphal, in the circumstances.

9

When Alice was a child she thought often about astronauts. She had seen images on television of the moon landing and the space walks, and found these endlessly fascinating. Astronauts were like another species, semihuman, given to slow-motion movement and weightless contingency. They were bluish, denatured, radically alone. She watched their bouncing movements on the moon and the pretend game of golf, the moon buggy, hurtling along, and the planting of a flag, and all these seemed to her a kind of phoney theatrics, designed to disguise the essential melancholy of their existence. The screened face Alice found especially sad: it was as if encasement in a helmet was certain erasure. It was almost scary – a visible emptiness, a shiny black cavity where the face should have been. A phantom might reside there, a technical spook. At the same time, space-walking astronauts resembled large babies. They had useless limbs and cumbrous gestures, their autonomic devices rendered them dependent, they seemed unborn, or just-born, or not quite fully made. Drifting in the dark of outer space, they were hardly believable. They bore a silvery, stroboscopic glow.

Her precocity enabled Alice to realise that the astronaut, in its many manifestations and with its contradicting attributes, somehow signified her sense of isolation. Norah was a popular girl, surrounded by chattering friends who embraced her, plaited her hair, gave her small pink gifts and trivial love notes, invited her to sleep-overs and doted on her skill at drawing ponies; but Alice was separate and remote, with only cleverness to recommend her. Other girls found her intimidating. Boys, who wished always to court her favour, also mocked her for what they secretly admired: she could kick a football through the goalposts from any angle, she could do maths in her head, she had an ambition to windsurf. In the tribal community of school, where conformity was rewarded and talent was stringently controlled, Alice was a deviation, an exceptional child. She ate her lunch alone, and read books in the library while other students ran in screaming gangs around the playground or tumbled and wrestled on the huge grass oval.

Norah's popularity made Alice cruel, and Norah, in turn, learned to mock her sister, often to an audience. Gifted with mimicry of a range of voices and accents, Norah played out small dramas in which she retold *Alice in Wonderland*, implicating her sister in preposterous and humiliating situations. Alice discovered, to her dismay, that she had only one voice; she had no skill at all for dramatic improvisation. She developed a superstition that she had been given the wrong name, and that 'Norah', in fact, was her true definition. But no amount of persuasion or bullying caused Norah to relinquish 'Norah', and Alice was forced to endure the burden of pre-emptive fiction and the sting of her sister's persistent derision.

There had been a time, during Alice's bout of scarlet fever, when Norah had seemed both loving and concerned. Alice was then seven and Norah five, not yet a schoolgirl, not yet distinguished among her peers as an entertainer. At first Alice had been so ill she barely noticed Norah's response, the softness of her expression, the sisterly tokens – a handmade card featuring a smiling pony. She had watched her own slender body, from the face and neck down, gradually consumed by the tiny bumps of a startling, lurid rash, which in turn stung her and grew itchy and was unendurable. In the isolation ward, which she shared with James, her ears also ached and began leaking fluid; her fever had come and gone, so that she was at times insensible, and towards the end her crimson rash began to flake and peel away, so that she might have been a girl coming apart, a girl transmogrifying, a creature of some sort from *Grimm's Fairy Tales*.

For all this, the time in hospital was a revelation. Alice learned that machines have electrical lives, that there is a furtive inside to ordinary things. She learned that forces and ripples, numbers and systems, lie beneath actions and functions of every kind. And she learned, less directly, that Norah pressed her nose against the glass and was lovingly distraught at the sight of her hurt face and reddened body.

Norah remembered the isolation ward as the adventure she was locked out of. She was appalled by her sister's illness, but also unaware, as young children are, of its real physical danger. She saw Alice taken away, held apart, secured in a space of manifest suffering. Each time the family visited, Alice looked worse. Norah imagined that when she returned home she would be unrecognisable. A mixture of envy and fear governed her feelings. That her sister should be chosen like this, should be the object of such attention. That she had become coloured, damaged, that this illness might happen to her. Norah was overcome by confused and largely private feelings. She took her sister mandarins and comics, tributes from the outside world, but was ruled by a conviction that their separation was somehow permanent.

After the episode of illness, Alice grew closer to her father. She saw in him specialist knowledge and a daring trade. He carried the aura, or so she imagined, of a man who daily escaped electrocution, who dabbled in the coherent logic of currents and switches, who made machines work – washing machines, televisions, electric kettles, hot-water systems – and fixed lighting devices of every shape and form. He was a man who worked in silence, in a vault of self-enclosure, which Alice felt too that she admired and understood. When, for a time, he was employed by the Electrical Commission, climbing lampposts with a leather belt in the middle of wild storms, she heroicised him extravagantly. She saw him return, dripping wet, his face grimy and exhausted, and imagined how he had climbed in wind and rain to the top of a pole, engineered the resumption of current, looked with a challenge at the sky, and then descended, with only the modest attitude of a job well done. Pat hated her husband going out at night into storms. For her he was a lightning conductor, a man foolishly exposed, a man risking too much. After months of her anxiety, Fred left the Commission and returned to his job as an electrical contractor.

At weekends, Fred taught Alice how to kick a football. Norah was often away visiting friends, and Alice and her father entered into an easy companionship. She asked him electrical questions, which he never failed to answer, and he showed her the finer points of Australian Rules – marking, handballing, calculating the angle of opportunity in a shot for the goal. They watched matches together on television and he supplied the commentary, naming the players and estimating their talents, giving mini-histories of their league achievements, identifying past and future medal winners. Alice loved the way he shouted 'Yes!' when a goal was scored, raising his arms, flinging himself back in his chair in a physical code of approval. The action replay of each goal – from many angles and at variable speed – assured Alice of the mysterious relativity of vision. More than the fast-racing weather it proved that time was flexible, that technology ruled. Pat brought them sweet tea and chocolate biscuits, and the Saturday afternoon matches knitted together, season after season, becoming a sequence of mutuality and unspoken, everyday love. When Fred went outside to smoke, Alice followed him. She watched his large hands assemble a cigarette; she watched him lick the tissue paper and tap each end. She watched as he struck his match backwards and took his first puff. He would lean back, inhale and close his eyes.

In the patterns that families make, their fund of symmetry and asymmetry, Norah, perhaps predictably, became much closer to Pat. Alice watched her sister and mother bent at joint sewing projects – for which she had no interest at all – and heard their murmurous exchanges, which always sounded confidential and thick with special information. They cut female shapes out of cloth spread on the kitchen table, pinned them, tacked them, fashioned a garment. Each gave to sewing a focus and diligence Alice reserved only for reading novels. Perhaps these were not so dissimilar, she vaguely thought. The formless beginning, the following of line, the imagining of a body inside a shape, the final art, which one entered, fitted to oneself, made essentially one's own. She would have liked to test her analogy on her sister and mother, but this was not possible. Pat was a practical, no-nonsense woman whose preference between her daughters was clear. She was puzzled by Alice but charmed by Norah; felt troubled by this articulate wilful girl, and at ease with the genial younger child, whom other mothers liked, who was the kind of schoolgirl star she would herself have liked to be. Once, after witnessing Alice slaughter a kangaroo, Pat felt a revulsion she was unsure she would ever overcome. It was such a manly act, so peculiar for a girl. She had watched in the rear-view mirror as Alice lifted an axe, again and again. When she wanted to hurt her daughter, she mentioned the kangaroo, made her a criminal, invoked her permanent shame.

In grade six, students were asked to announce to the class what profession or occupation they wished to pursue as adults. Among the girls there were large populations of would-be hairdressers and air hostesses, a sprinkling of nurses, teachers and movie stars. Alice said in a loud voice that she wanted to be an astronaut and a windsurfer. A hoot went up amongst the boys, and the girls giggled in chorus. The teacher, a woman in her fifties with a sour, tired face, told her that she was 'unrealistic' and Alice knew immediately that her confession would fuel a new round of mockery. By afternoon Norah had heard the story from her classmates and she left an ugly drawing of a puffy astronaut in Alice's school bag. It bore the caption 'Wonderland Martian finally returns home'. Alice staunchly refused to cry. But she hated her sister for marking so explicitly her sense of outlandish estrangement, her habitual pomposity, her inability to fit. She hated the way others worked to determine and constrain her, and her sister's collaboration in discipline and control.

In her fifteenth year, Alice re-met Norah. They liked each other. More than that, each at last acknowledged the specificity of the other, their unequivocal, even strident, and separate characters. Although they looked nothing alike — Alice was fair and blue-eyed, Norah dark, like her father — they asserted a kind of interior affinity, a sisterly wisdom. It invigorated each, this at-last communion. That first summer of sisterhood they spent long days at the beach, swimming in the ocean, lying on their bellies on the sand, discussing novels, body-surfing waves, floating face up, eyes closed, somewhere between Australia and Africa. It occurred to Alice later, as an adult, that all families have these enclosed and radiant periods, these nests of delight almost too easily achieved to be acknowledged, that come on holidays, or weekends, or summers by the beach, and that, however fleeting or tenuous or finally unstable, form the nostalgia of redeeming memory. There were no happy families, all alike, or unhappy families, tragically distinctive, but blendings of each, patched compositions. So it was between siblings, who moved in and out of contact, and parents and children, who shared immense histories, in which nothing was irrelevant, but learn and relearn, and then relearn again, how to get on in the demanding present.

Among the forms of her newly discovered devotion, Norah accompanied Alice to her windsurfing lessons. The sails were heavy and Alice failed again and again. No exertion seemed strong enough to stabilise the board. The instructor recommended daily push-ups and back-strengthening exercises. Five months later, when Alice was finally able to catch the wind, to move across the river like a skimming bird, Norah applauded. As Alice flew for the first time into the crimson glow of late afternoon, she heard her sister on the shore, shouting and cheering, as a boy might at a football match. Infinity opened before her. The great snake of the river wrinkled beneath her board; she felt the thrill of velocity and the pleasure of riding between elements, sliding in a rare, lonesome, space. Sky seemed to be everywhere. It slanted around her. Yet it was not astronautical; it was all direction and speed. It was the body almost naked, lashed by spray and tutored by wind. When she surfed, motion accelerated, as it does in a movie, and when she fell into the water, there was the shock of overall sensation and a struggle to stay afloat and gain control.

Once she had learned to windsurf, Alice grew more confident. It was as if, in achieving this skill, she had confirmed the plausibility of 'unrealistic' ambition and the heady expansiveness of day-to-day things. She inhabited her own body with strength and an intimation of its pleasures. She walked with a stride. She argued with her teachers. She could also win an arm-wrestle with almost any boy at school, and only later understood that this was a kind of sexual engagement.

When Alice gained entrance to university, on a government scholarship, her parents were clearly both pleased and alarmed. University learning sounded to each of them essentially unnecessary, an excess, or a trifle. Fred surveyed with mistrust Alice's handbook of units, and asked her dismissive and prickly questions. In some way, she realised, he felt betrayed. He would have liked her to be a shop assistant, married to a footballer. He worried that she would no longer speak to him, that he would seem a bore, an old man, a superannuated worker. Alice watched his large hands flick through the university guide, pausing indiscriminately, as he read aloud a title or a unit description.

'Electrical engineering; here's one I could do.'

Behind his reading glasses his eyes looked rheumy and smudged, his face abraded. He had developed a habit of running his fingers through his thinning hair. It was true, he was growing old. There is always a memorable moment when one's parents first appear truly old; for Alice it was here, as Fred expressed his undignified resentment in the movements of his hands, the tone of his voice, the way he flung the handbook before him when he had finished with it, in the way, most of all, he appeared collapsed, threatened, by so small a text and so weighty a symbol.

Fred remembered at this time – for no particular reason – the day Alice and Norah had found the whale skeleton. They had been gone for hours, and he and Pat were frantic with worry. He had searched up and down the beach for their towels, fearing both were drowned. Then, when he had returned to report to Pat another failure to find them, there they were, running up the sand hill, flushed with excitement and rosy with sunburn. They wore identical yellow sundresses, which Pat had sewn, and were a picture of unreasonable, girlish excitement. He had spoken harshly, shouting at them, shouting out all of his accumulated anxiety. And when he had finished shouting, they told him of the skeleton. They were each so pleased with their discovery, so sure it was extraordinary, that they seemed not to comprehend their parents' anger, or to admit it. Alice persuaded Fred to return with them, to retrieve a bone.

'Imagine,' she said, 'bones as big as a house. Just there. Just for us. Shining on the sand.'

Pat insisted the girls stay in the beach hut as a punishment, but Fred gave in. He followed his two daughters, who seemed, unusually, to be in a state of truce, back along the beach, beyond the far cove, into the little bay where the skeleton rested.

It was — he knew it immediately — a beautiful thing. He could see the girls' footprints all around, and curving in the centre. They had played here; they had claimed it. It looked charmed, pure. Fred reached up high and wrested a spinal bone free. It was wing-shaped and porous-looking. The girls held one end of the shape and he the other, and with the object between them, this unburied treasure, they began the long, slow walk back, sharing the weight all together.

Within a few months of beginning university, Alice left home. It would be easier to be a university student, she told herself, away from her family. She shared a house with four others, two women and two men, and they lived in the disorganised, down-at-heel squalor that typically characterises student accommodation. Alice felt liberated, but she also felt lost. Unused to the social regimes of people her age, the turbulence of parties and drinking sessions, the hours-long dope-smoking and the ponderousness it brought in its wake, she began to retreat to her room, turning once again inward. To be alone she spent whole days on the river, surfing in all weathers, when she should have been attending lectures. Eventually she used her scholarship money to rent an apartment on her own, a single room. It was a spell she entered, a sudden relief. She studied, had love affairs, played her own music. She came and went as she pleased, and answered to no one.

When Norah visited, Alice cooked her elaborate Indian meals and they talked together with a new and vigorous energy, as if each otherwise lived in solitary confinement. Norah was impatient to finish school and enter art college. She missed her sister. She asked her to phone more frequently. They talked deep into the night, lingering with pleasure over the restorative anecdote, the casual perception, the trailing conversation, wayward and fortuitous, that led to the genuine intersections and exchanges between them. Alice imagined their voices as silky ribbons, blown out of the window, across roads and roofs, to fly like a gauzy banner above the restless river.

10

Let me tell you, *wrote Mr Sakamoto*, about John Logie
Baird, the inventor of television. (An artifice of
modernity I confess especially to like, despite the fact
that it is without the qualities of nuance and eternity.)

Another Scotsman of dogged ingenuity and
generous humanity, he was born in 1888, the fourth
child of Jessie and the Reverend John Baird, in the little
town of Helensburgh, just west of Glasgow. From an
early age he was accident-prone, and both ill and
inventive in full measure. A boy of conspicuous
leadership, he devised telephonic communication and
electric lighting for his friends, and almost killed
himself being launched in a home-made glider from the
high gabled roof of his parents' house. The vehicle
broke in half, depositing him, in his own words, 'with a
terrific bump on the lawn' and left behind a life-long
fear of flying.

He was at first a mediocre student, and studied
electrical engineering at technical college, gaining a
diploma before he could be admitted to Glasgow
University, where, as it happens, he never finished his
degree. But already, as a young man, Baird was
imagining technologies of vision – imagining

reflection, scanning, radar, display. He was already producing the poetically named 'shadowgraphs', grey blurry outlines of images on screens. Transmission excited him, focus, clarity. In his small laboratory in Soho, London, he worked with a dummy's head, sharpening the image, experimenting with photoelectric cells; and then one day, there it was, sure as the nose on his face. Baird ran downstairs, seized an office boy by the elbow, and paid him two shillings and sixpence to stand where the dressmaker's dummy had stood. So he saw before him, now, a distinctive human face, electrically transmitted. It was 1925. The boy, William Taynton – Bill to his friends – was dematerialised and represented in a stream of light.

Television was first publicly demonstrated in January 1926. Short of funds, Baird had learned to employ unconventional materials. To create his mechanical scanning device, which required spinning discs, he used several hatboxes mounted on a coffin lid. The images were tiny – no more than visiting-card size – and limited to head and shoulder shots. Even so, it was a marvel. The first television was this contraption of assorted and incongruous objects – like something Marcel Duchamp might construct, like a surrealist object combining, symbolically at least, death and art – and these miniature rectangles, these impossible windows. Who would have foreseen then, in 1926, that impossible seeing would become habitual, domestic, addictive and omnipresent, that it would gain mystifying supremacy and uncontested power, that moon walks, assassinations, cyclones and pop divas would appear in lounge rooms across the globe with a kind of facile unanimity?

Unlike Bell, Baird did not become a multimillionaire.

He held on too long to the model of mechanical vision, only converting to the cathode-ray tube receiver, the future of television, in 1932. He was in relentless dispute with the Marconi Wireless Telegraph Company and the Bell Telephone Company of America who, with more money, developed his ideas beyond his control. Baird's technology was also taken up by the state – the BBC. His own early efforts went towards producing cinema television, the broadcast, on a large screen, of celebrities and horse races. The Second World War also halted his research and jeopardised the fortunes of his relatively small company. He died in 1946, mourned by a loving family, but under-recognised for his genius.

Photographs of John Logie Baird show a remarkably handsome man. But he never looks at the camera. He gazes far away, at a more vigilant lens, one that sees and transports faces with more lavish compulsion, telecasts them dramatically, from aerials and satellites, carries them hither and thither, over vast, vast distances.

*

Outside it was raining. The drains thundered and gurgled. The building opposite – offices, Alice supposed – had a slick and darkened appearance, more sombre now since Leo, and the police, and the leaving of flowers. The mini-memorial had disappeared, but Alice was not sure when, or by whom, it had been dismantled. One day she noticed it was no longer there.

'There,' said Alice, pointing. 'He was left in that doorway.'

Mr Sakamoto followed the line of her arm.

'The students don't congregate here any more. They've found a new spot, further up the street. So I no longer see Gisele and Sylvain, Arlette and the others, except in glimpses, from a distance.'

'They needed to move,' Mr Sakamoto said simply.

Alice wondered if she did. Every time she stepped outside she still thought: this is where Leo died. This is where a young man living in his headphones, in his own world of sound, was beaten to death in the early evening, with no one noticing. She imagined there was a kind of residue in the air, a trace of wickedness or defilement. She imagined she could smell blood.

Alice and Mr Sakamoto were sharing coffee in her studio. It was a new stage of friendship, a new form of trust. In the air sounded the soft syncopation of the rain, a sound tender and appropriate to the oblique quality of their feelings.

Mr Sakamoto looked relaxed and introspective.

'I had a phone call today. From the past. From Clare.'

Alice could tell he had been waiting to announce this news.

'Clare?'

'The woman I told you about. In the bookshop. In Edinburgh.'

'Ah, that Clare. How many years is it?'

'Actually, I met her again only last year. I was back in Edinburgh, researching Bell. I was working in the Scottish National Library, reading, somewhat laboriously, the curious verses and philosophies of his grandfather, Alexander, and when I raised my face for a break she was standing before me. Apart from her grey hair she looked much the same – still slim and attractive, still slightly Japanese. She wore a maroon velvet jacket and a black woollen scarf, dangling loose, as if she had just come in from the cold outside. We were awkward with each other, unsure what to say. Clare sat in the seat opposite – I think she was sizing me up, wondering what she saw in me all those years ago – and then she suggested we go out for a drink. We talked about old times, our children – she has two, and four grandchildren – she spoke of the death of her husband. I said a little about Mie, not very much, and bragged at length about Akiko and Haruko. We exchanged addresses and telephone numbers, and there was one of those wistful, hesitant moments, just as we parted. I leaned forward and kissed her on the cheek; she responded with an embrace.'

Mr Sakamoto paused.

'That night I dreamed about Mie, and woke myself grieving. I hadn't dreamed about her for years, not since her death. It was a perplexing thing. Like being hauled backwards. This is one thing I should have learned by now: that grief never finishes . . . Anyway, Clare rang me early this morning. She must have phoned Haruko – one of the numbers on my card – she had given her the telephone number of my hotel.'

'What did Clare want?'

'It was one of those long-distance calls where the caller speaks too loudly, and cannot settle easily into conversation. In any case, she said she was about to begin travelling and wanted to meet. She said she knew I wouldn't be in Japan, but was surprised to find me so close – as it were – just across the channel. She'll be here next week.'

Alice was waiting, not sure what Mr Sakamoto wanted her to say. They both listened to the rain, which seemed to be easing. Rain is also unmodern, Alice was thinking, so messy, importunate.

'I was going to ask,' he went on, 'if you'd have dinner with us. It would make it easier, I think. Less potentially romantic . . .'

'Ah, so you're scared of her?'

'Yes. Well, no. I just don't want her to get the wrong idea . . .'

Mr Sakomoto smiled. He looked younger, not dressed in his suit and tie.

Alice was pleased he had asked for her protection. It was as if they were old friends, as if what lay between them was known, secure. The compact of familiarity, its reassurance.

'I'd be delighted,' Alice responded.

Their talk drifted to topics of books and literature. Mr Sakamoto said that reading had saved his life. Not mathematics. Not money. Not travel. Reading. At a time, he said, when he felt blasted by images, words had anchored him, secured him, stopped his free-falling plunge into nowhere.

Alice bent her head. Mr Sakamoto's voice was calm and serious. Outside the rain had ceased. The world was shining wet. They would step out together, walk the paved, puddled region along the river, then part, each to their own projects, each back to the silent production of words.

*

Alice realised that she and her mother had never spoken. They had talked, of course, traded pragmatic conversation and even pleasurable repartee, but there was no occasion on which they had sat down, woman to woman, and encountered each other in the full density of their fraught relationship. Pat was ashamed of Alice, but Alice was not sure why. There was a fissure, a chasm, that neither could cross. What Alice knew of her mother she had learned from her grandmother, Vera, and from conjecture based on the slightly brown snaps in the family photograph album. Pat had suffered four miscarriages before Alice arrived. There had been this protracted and repeated emptying out, this negative awareness of the body, this expectation of disaster. Vera said that at first Pat had been depressed, but by the fourth pregnancy was in a state of numb resignation. She said nothing of Alice's birth, or any subsequent rejoicing. Perhaps, Alice reasoned, Pat was by then less interested in babies, cautious and pessimistic. In photographs of Alice's babyhood she was depicted, disproportionately, in her father's arms; Pat was the photographer, it seemed. Or she had given over the child, set up a substitute parent, so that any new loss would not destroy her.

Before her marriage Pat worked in a pharmacy store. She had left school at fifteen to support her widowed mother, and found a position almost immediately at Drakes, in Burt Street. Vera insisted she had tried to persuade her daughter to stay at school – 'a real bright spark, real brainy, your mum, could've done anything'. But Pat was worried about her mother's inadequate pension and determined to help. She had two younger brothers, Harry and Ted, and both stayed on and completed their schooling.

Work in the pharmacy suited her. There was the vaguely glamorous aspect to selling cosmetics, which Pat, for whom cinema was a pre-eminent pleasure, adored, and she also learned the rudiments of organic chemistry from her employer, Mr Drake. So she was able to try lipstick samples – she settled on 'Sunset Rose', her life-long choice – but also to study, in an *ad hoc* way, the world of chemical combinations and medicinal advice. She was proud of her work; she felt her knowledge a genuine achievement. Miners' wives invariably wanted something for coughs, something to counter the wretched dissolution of their husbands' lungs, but even Pat knew that there were conditions a simple prescription could not alleviate. She watched distraught women leave, clutching their brown paper bags. The new drills in the mine were popularly called 'widow makers': they sent tiny blades and splinters of quartz straight into the throat. The unions were agitating; there had never been so much illness.

By the time Pat met Fred she was desperate for romance.

Hollywood had given her an expectation of dramatic interventions and the irresistible swerving of life into the arms of a strong man. She dreamed of slippery satin dresses and kisses accompanied by music. At the Firemen's Ball Fred was notable for his quiet self-composure. He was not nervously searching the room for a partner, nor did he seem lonely or lacking in confidence. He was also tall, dark and handsome. She heard a man's voice address him with affection as Blackie. When he walked towards her and asked her to dance, she had already decided: yes, he's the one.

They both wanted children. But trying became a series of tragic disappointments and after ten years it seemed almost impossible. Pat gazed at other women's children and went home to weep. Then there were two babies, in just two years. Alice and Norah were both feisty girls, who fought from the beginning, even as infants. Pat laboured over making them matching frilly outfits and dainty accessories, as if this would somehow guarantee a likeness or accord, but the girls shamed her by their shouting matches and bad behaviour. Alice was mostly to blame, being the oldest. Alice shattered Pat's image of herself as the mother of pretty, presentable daughters. Alice was wayward and wilful. She pinched Norah at every opportunity and even wanted to take her name.

As they grew, Pat became much closer to Norah. It was inevitable, she thought. They sat side by side at the Singer sewing machine, feeding lengths of cloth beneath its speedy needle. Their shoulders touched. Pat watched her elder daughter proclaim at family gatherings that she wanted to be an astronaut, while Norah, who resembled her father and was darkly beautiful, attracted others by the force of her personality alone. She was popular at school and elected School Captain. Pat saw in her the success she automatically esteemed. Yet even with Norah there was distance and unbreachable estrangement. Pat felt profoundly the solitary history of her body, her four lost babies, weighing somewhere inside her, like a persistent despondency. Her breasts sagged with the downward pull of her maternal history. She was old at thirty. She was sorrowful and embittered. Fred seemed unchanged by their marriage, and she was unable to tell him how very altered she was. Every marriage has these silences, these demolitions. The white noise of interior monologues that can never be spoken.

When Alice gained admission to the university, Pat felt something for her daughter approximating admiration, but did not think to tell her. The University. It was where rich kids went. It was where young men and women learned subjects she could barely pronounce. She was not sure what it was that Alice was studying, but liked to be able to say, 'my eldest, Alice, she's now at the University'. When Alice visited on Sundays she saw that Pat liked her more now she had moved out of home. As she sat with Fred, watching football highlights he had videotaped from Saturday's *Match of the Day*, Pat hovered, offering drinks and making polite conversation. Sometimes she smiled at her daughter as one would to a friendly stranger. It was a tentative peace between them, after all these years. Once she reached over and stroked her daughter's hair. Alice looked up, surprised. Her touch was so unfamiliar.

*

In the internet café, everyone but Alice seemed to be smoking. The air was miasmic, foul. She felt she was suffocating. The two rows of computer monitors, back to back, were ablaze in the carcinogenic dimness. At each sat someone under forty, typing intently or scrolling their mouse between ferocious puffs, for which the management had thoughtfully provided ashtrays in the shape of fish. When she looked along the row Alice saw Google, Hotmail, Yahoo, pornography, chat-sites and something that appeared to be an online casino: it flashed 'Money! Money! Money!' in a circle of rotating lights.

This was an odd form of consumption, or play, or technological subservience, to be seated at the receptive nexus of so many intervening sites. There were galaxies of information in there, illimitable networks more complex than neural pathways, zapping multidirectionally. There were people to be met and goods to be bought. There were bodies to see and information to be known. Any book was there, to be sped towards you. Any crazy notion or marginal subgroup, any egoistic individual or antiquarian hobby. *The mind of God.* Cluttered, schismatic, astronomical, microscopic.

Alice felt depressed. After this, she thought, she would visit a bookshop. Her tastes in knowledge garnering were irredeemably old-fashioned. She loved the feel of books, their integrity as objects. The wing-plan of them, the scent and warmth of paper. She loved the relative stiffness of the cover and the sentience of settled print. Random flicking of pages, inscriptions, dog-ears. She loved – though it was a sin – to see books left open upside down, their bird shape accentuated in the keeping of a page. She loved those images of the Annunciation in which the Virgin rests her index finger on a page of her book, retaining her place during Gabriel's visit. Or the mortuary statues in European churches, that have dukes and bishops sleeping in death on the pillow of an open book. She loved second-hand bookshops for their presumption that any tatty volume mattered, and new bookshops, for their signs and neat rows of books, waiting to be opened for the very first time. Inherited books. Books as gifts. Books as objects flung across the room in a lover's argument. Books (this most of all) taken into the warm sexual space of the bed, held upon the lap, entered like another body, companionable, close, interconnecting with innermost things. Those bed books that chart the route between waking and sleeping, that are a venture of almost hypnagogic power. Those enticements. Adventures. Corridors of words. Capsules. Secrets.

Alice's e-mail announcement said she had fifty-one new messages. When she dragged the cursor over the list, only four were personal; another seven were from the university. The others sold sex aids, pharmaceuticals, land in the Bahamas, invited her to increase her dick size, to look at Mandy, to order a pet mongoose – delivered within two days – online with her credit card. From Stephen there was a long e-mail that began formally and with great restraint, but transmuted as it developed into a stream-of-consciousness rave, accusing her of severity and lack of feeling. E-mails generated stray emotion and haphazard expression. They had a viral susceptibility that altered tone. Cynical hip-dialect, datastream waywardness. It distressed Alice to read Stephen's note, and it was almost unanswerable. She would have to fashion a self-defence, find words that recovered the initial formality and refused the hysterical machinic transference. It was laborious, writing to Stephen, but he would be waiting for a reply, checking his in-box several times a day. E-mail functioned in this way, too, to give imperative demand, or command, where none should have existed.

Among other messages was one from her mother, who had only recently acquired an internet connection. Pat's letter read as if it had been delivered from another era: it had none of the typos, contractions and poor punctuation of e-mail, but was thoughtful, measured and composed with care. 'Dear Alice, how are you? I hope you are well.' Alice remembered being taught in primary school that a letter should begin in this way. It was touching, this sentimental holding to form. Her mother wrote that Fred needed another hernia operation, but was otherwise cheerful and still preoccupied with his garden. She said nothing of Norah, or Michael, but mentioned that she minded the children for a period each day, and found them exhausting. She was as usual, she said. 'I'm just the same, the same as usual.' Alice leaned back in her chair and thought about her mother, typing with slow and careful progress this almost uninflected letter. There was nothing of Pat, no trace of the personification that often surges into the e-mails, unwithheld by constraints of correct expression, driven by speed, birthed by the cyberspatial illusion of unaccountability. Avoiding e-mail laxities, Pat avoided genuine disclosure.

Alice replied tersely, saying that she would ring on Sunday. Around her, other internet clients stared into their cubes of light, arranged liaisons, gambled money, looked deep into the gaping bodies of strangers, sent business messages to the distant ends of the globe. The man sitting next to her downloaded a tourist map of Cuba. The room was thick with information, with webs, with licit and illicit connections, with precipitous surplus. Alice lurched out into the drizzling rain and took a deep breath. She raised her umbrella and without pausing, dashed dangerously into the traffic. She was three streets away before she realised she had forgotten to log out.

Mr Sakamoto said later that Alice made no sense, that one could not love technology and hate the internet. It was a logical contradiction.

'I am large enough,' Alice responded, 'to contain contradictions.'

Mr Sakamoto laughed.

'Let me tell you', he said, 'about the *kamishibai* man. When my daughters were little, there still existed in Japan a few *kamishibai* men, oral storytellers who went from village to village on bicycles. Our *kamishibai* man arrived by train and set himself up at the local library, but essentially he still performed the same function. He held up sequences of cards, which formed the basis of his story. Sometimes he had notes on the back of each card; sometimes he simply knew from practice what to say. The children were entranced. It was a delightful combination of image and voice — black ink line drawings of great sensitivity, and this man — whose name we never discovered — playing with a range of voices, stretching into a high falsetto and sinking into a low rumble.'

'And the connection with the internet?'

'No connection, really. My point is that the *kamishibai* man existed alongside television and movies and other forms of storytelling. Nothing is lost. There are no cataclysmic displacements or the sudden vanishing of forms. Books still exist. Millions of people still read them. Perhaps even *kamishibai* men still exist . . .'

*

Alice was swimming laps in the interior pool at Les Halles. Although she walked miles around the city, she needed this immersion, this strenuous repetition of arms and legs, striving, going nowhere. Under the fluorescent lights the surface of the water looked oily, with an iridescent sheen that her body broke, and broke again. Its blue was startling, a Grecian indigo. Tiles, artfully deceitful, created this false Aegean, this jet-setter's hue. The stench of chlorine was making Alice feel dizzy. She listened to herself in the water, heard her lungs filling and emptying, the huff and puff of her exercise. When she lifted her head the muffled amplification of the pool thundered around her. Down, back into the body. Up, the clang of a shout reverberating between the walls, the rise and fall of voices, the almost clattering sound of a splash. She could not have explained her hypersensitivity. As she worked her arms and legs like a machine, she heard more than anything her organic self, her blood, her breath, her heaving body, and felt a vague distress, as if she were crying in the water. Her black swimsuit rode up and clung tight, and with her thumbs she pulled it down and snapped it around her buttocks. She stopped, and trod water. All of a sudden she knew. She was missing windsurfing. The wet body that rises and flies away, straight towards the horizon. The labour of muscles, straining and feeling tight for a pull towards the sky, and the flash of a sheath of light, suddenly descending.

II

When they returned to the bistro, the two waiters greeted Mr Sakamoto with kisses and exclamations. It was as if he were a sit-com hero, who solves the problems by the end of an episode, and is then regarded with demonstrative affection by his fellow players. Alice heard herself introduced as 'a fine young scholar from Australia', and then she too was enjoined in this magic circle. The older of the waiters, Jacques, fussed and hung around, promising a *spécialité*, pouring them an aperitif neither really wanted. The waiters were reunited. Mr Sakamoto was Cupid, they said, responsible for their reunion. When he bowed, they returned his bow, pleased to be implicated in his world of ceremonious thoughtfulness.

Over lunch he expressed nervous anticipation about Clare. Her arrival was imminent – at the end of the week – and he felt she was coming under false pretences, that he had told her of his lonely widower's life and she had imagined romance. After two aperitifs and a glass of wine, however, Mr Sakamoto's nervousness fled. He became voluble and cheery.

'I suppose we could always travel together for a while,' he told Alice. 'Get to know one another. See what happens . . .'

He seemed to be asking her advice.

The noise in the bistro rose in a sudden roar. A large group of businessmen were celebrating something. They toasted with arms upraised and slapped one another's backs. They all had loosened ties and alcoholic expressions. Two men were simultaneously shouting into mobile phones.

'I've been wondering —' said Alice, leaning closer, 'just to change the subject — about the *kamishibai* man. Can you tell me one of his stories?'

'They are stories for children,' Mr Sakamoto said.

'I know. But to give me some idea.'

Mr Sakamoto stirred his truffle spaghetti, the *spécialité*, offered as a gift. 'Excellent,' he said, gesturing with his fork.

'For Akiko and Haruko there was a favourite story, one they wished to hear again and again. It's a famous Japanese folktale about a Princess of Bamboo. Once upon a time, there was an old man and his wife — a childless and virtuous peasant couple. One day the old man went to the bamboo grove to collect edible shoots, and saw there a bamboo stem illuminated in the middle. A white light shone with great radiance from within the plant. Curious to know what was inside, he carefully cut the bamboo and was astonished to find there a tiny baby, small enough to rest in the palm of his hand. He took the baby home, and he and his wife raised it as their own. The baby grew to become an extraordinarily beautiful woman, a woman graceful and good. (In the drawings she wore a kimono with a bamboo print and her long hair was loose and thick, resting on her back down to her waist.) Suitors came from all over Japan to propose marriage to the Bamboo Princess. However, she refused all offers, and became very sad, crying every day. Her parents were upset, but their daughter would not explain the nature or cause of her sadness. She became thin and pale, but of course remained very beautiful.'

Here Mr Sakamoto paused to take large mouthfuls of his spaghetti, and a sip of red wine.

'One night, a night of full moon, the Bamboo Princess told her parents she was crying because she had to return to her home in the moon. She had been delaying her departure, but now the time had come. Rays of moonbeam stretched down to transport her home. She embraced her old parents and gave them the elixir of life. Then she left, waving. There were lovely drawings of her ascension – a kind of path of light, a ray, pulling her upwards. In Japan we have a traditional reverence for the moon. And for bamboo, as well. I used to think that my daughters liked the story because it is about escaping one's parents, but Haruko told me when she grew up that they both liked the idea of a princess living in the moon. Haruko used to talk to her, she said, in a private conversation. They could see her face, up there, somewhere in the moon.'

Mr Sakamoto resumed his meal. 'Excellent,' he said again.

These precious stories, Alice was thinking. These clandestine histories of children, sewn with patches of fantasy, spaced out, far-fetched, bold in their childish strangeness.

'You're quiet today,' Mr Sakamoto said. He was twirling the final forkful of his special spaghetti.

'I was thinking about children.'

'Ah.'

'And about the moon. Did you know that since Apollo ɪɪ the moon is covered with footprints? And because there is no wind on the moon, no rain, no erosion, no kind of agitation, the footprints will stay there, undisturbed, for millennia to come. It troubles me, this defacement. The surface of the moon, the *face* of the moon, trampled, stamped by ridged boots.'

Mr Sakamoto wiped his plate with a piece of bread and then threw it into his mouth with satisfying conclusiveness. He swallowed the bread in a gulp, and with another finished his wine. Alice thought to herself that he ate like an Italian gangster in a movie. She had rarely seen him eat with such pleasure.

'I didn't know that,' he said. 'You make it sound like a violation.'

'Think of it,' insisted Alice. 'Footprints by the thousand on the Sea of Tranquillity.' She bent over her meal, conscious that Mr Sakamoto was sitting back in his chair, sated.

'About Clare,' he began.

'See how it goes on Friday. Make a decision then.'

'That's what Uncle Tadeo said.'

As if on cue, Mr Sakamoto's mobile telephone rang. The opening bars of the 1812 Overture, in a trilling version, sounded absurdly loud.

'*Moshi, Moshi?*'

It was Uncle Tadeo, having a sleepless night. Alice listened to Mr Sakamoto's Japanese voice. He spoke in a low, regular and solicitous tone, even though it sounded to her a mountainous language, full of peaks and valleys, of rises and declensions. Unable to recognise a single word, Alice tried to imagine Uncle Tadeo – perhaps sitting up in bed, propped by large pillows, under ivory lamplight, his thin hair mussed from tossing and turning, the receiver clamped to his ear, listening with an old man's concentration to a beloved voice, Hiroshi's voice, travelling from day in Paris to night in Tokyo, contracting the globe in no time at all.

*

Let me tell you, *wrote Mr Sakamoto*, about Guglielmo Marconi, inventor of the wireless. This is a story of the triumph of the letter 'S' and of frills of sound waves sent spinning into the air.

Marconi was of a noble family, his father an Italian gentleman, his mother an Irish aristocrat, and when he came bawling into the world in 1874 he broadcast his existence to all Bologna. His parents were delighted. In Italy, as in Japan, a hefty cry is the sign of a full-blooming life. A hefty cry is a celebration. Of lungs sucking energy. Of inspiration. Later, as an adult, Marconi became soft-spoken. As befits a man of his class, a man who has ingrained in his manner the confidence of wealth and a private education, he bore advantages that meant that the slightest assertion of voice would be attended to and taken notice of. He was a refined fellow, both Irish and Italian in his good looks, of elegant dress, and calm, fastidious manner. His centre-parted hair was always neat, his manicured fingernails were clean as a whistle. Women noticed the moony cuticles and slender fingers (since women then, as today, were always remarking on the attractiveness of men's hands).

At only twenty-six years old Marconi patented the principle of 'syntonic telegraph', wireless communication. He designed a transmitter to send, and a receiver to detect, waves of radio. In the air was babble, data, rippling messages. They needed only to be dialled into audible existence, electromagnetically. Wires were base, material, tangled redundancies. But the gathering of waves, that was a new captivation; that was as beautiful as philosophy. It was as though the air was revealed in its mazed potentiality. It was like hearing angels. A pair of lovely hands twitched at knobs and adjusted valves. Crystals were set in place, amplifiers, coils. Marconi launched his own signals and sifted the air for their return.

And the letter 'S'? In December 1901, determined to prove that wireless waves were not affected by the curvature of the earth, Marconi set up a system across the Atlantic, stretching between Cornwall and

Newfoundland. The receiver in Canada used a coherer, a glass tube filled with iron filings, to conduct radio waves, and a balloon was employed to lift the antenna as high as possible. The message sent was the letter 'S', in Morse code. Marconi was jubilant. This was an epochal discovery. After this success he investigated radar, short waves and microwaves, the whole epiphenomena of the tingling skies.

Guglielmo Marconi received so many honours and awards that he died, it is said, of ornamentation. Among the most prestigious: the Nobel Prize for Physics, the Albert Medal of the Royal Society, the John Fritz Medal, the Kelvin Medal, the Order of St Anne (from the Tsar of Russia), the Commander of the Order of St Maurice and St Lazarus and the Grand Cross of the Order of the Crown of Italy (from the King of Italy), the Freedom of the City of Rome, Chevalier of the Civil Order of Savoy, Senatore of the Italian Senate, Honorary Knight Grand Cross of the Royal Victorian Order . . . and finally the hereditary title of Marchese. No man can endure this much accolade. Celebrity exhausted and finally killed him. We must imagine that in death Marconi's hands were folded in a tidy V on his chest, released at last from all that fidgeting with radiophonic components in the search for ruffles of sound, those exquisite tides.

*

On her eleventh birthday, Norah tried, with her hands in a W, to strangle her older sister. She was wearing a party dress, newly sewn, in tangerine and violet. It had a kind of pop art design and she thought it hideous. Alice teased and tormented her. They were preparing for a party, setting the table with bowls of food composed almost wholly of salt and sugar when, with an energy that surprised them both, Norah knocked Alice to the floor. She leaped upon Alice's prone body and grasped her throat with both hands. It was not play, or jest, but serious violence. Alice saw Norah's face swell and redden and felt her own throat collapse and her eyes spring tears. Their faces were very close; they stared at each other. Norah's lips were pursed, as if she were threading a needle. Alice pushed at her shoulders, but the weight of anger was too heavy, too imperative, to dislodge.

This is stupid, Alice thought, as she gasped and choked for air.

It may have been only seconds, but for each sister it was an extended and brutal moment, one that would follow them into the future as an unimaginable outrage. Fred appeared from nowhere and seized Norah from behind, pulling her away. Alice saw a flash of tangerine and violet as she took a deep breath. Her father's hands shook. He appeared to be trembling with distress. He sent Norah to her room and bent to lift Alice and inspect her throat. She too was sent away to her room. When Norah's friends arrived and the party began, Alice did not join them. She lay on her bed weeping, not from any pain, but from something intimately wrong that had no name. She could hear Norah receiving gifts with giggling chatter, and the high-pitched tones of girlish excitement. She could hear paper unwrapping and objects admired. Life was continuing without her. People were happy. Pat appeared at Alice's doorway with her hands on her hips and told her not to sulk, that if she wasn't careful she would miss the ice cream and jelly. Then without waiting for a reply or explanation, she turned and left.

The misery of a thirteen-year-old girl has a kind of ferocity. It is a consuming darkness, a simple warped thing. Alice felt hurt and ridiculous. She felt unloved. For all her heterodox assertions and eccentric ambitions, she knew too that she was composed of these disintegrating possibilities. Beyond her room children were singing 'Happy Birthday' and photographs were being taken. There was the exaggerated gaiety of hyped-up voices, a squeal here and there, a jolly call. When the song had concluded and the cheers had died away, Fred knocked gently and called through the door: 'A cuppa tea about now, what do you think?'

'Thanks,' Alice called back.

He had come to rescue her. In all that had happened and in the extremity of her feelings, this fatherly gesture was a deep consolation. Alice dried her eyes and looked at herself in the mirror. Her face swam there, bleary and immaterial. She wondered what she would look like as an adult. If she would be more solid. If, behind the mask of an astronaut's visor, she would be untouchable and stare down at the world like a god. Space opened before her. Stars. Galaxies. She would float away. They would all miss her terribly.

When Fred brought in a cup of tea and a slice of birthday cake, they sat on the bed together, side by side, and jointly regretted they were missing the big match. It was a quarter-final. Their team was not playing, but all week they had discussed the possible outcome and the shuffling of names and rankings on the competition ladder.

Alice lay her head in her father's lap. He brushed back her fringe and kissed her forehead.

*

Mr Sakamoto kept looking at his watch. Clare was almost twenty minutes late.

'She's not coming,' he said, adjusting his tie.

'She'll come.'

Alice was keen to reassure him. In the restaurant he was

perceptibly nervous. He had begun pleating the tablecloth and straightening the cutlery. Curious waiters glanced in their direction. Around them was the murmurous sound of other people dining, of knives tapping plates and glasses chinking, conversation between mouthfuls, low and courteous.

When she walked through the door, Alice knew Clare immediately from Mr Sakamoto's description. She had, indeed, a slightly Japanese face, and long grey hair held at the back with a clip. She wore a tawny cashmere dress and an overcoat she removed as she walked towards them. Alice thought she looked interesting.

'Sorry,' she said as she sat down, afluster. 'Got lost, would you believe it?'

Clare leaned across the table and shook Alice's hand.

'Clare Keely,' she said.

There was no apparent surprise at Alice's presence. Perhaps Mr Sakamoto had told Clare of his guest.

'Well, here we are.'

'Here we are,' Mr Sakamoto repeated.

They smiled at each other. Small talk ensued, talk about the efficiency of the Métro, the volatile weather, the physical changes evident in Paris. As the meal proceeded, Mr Sakamoto began to relax.

'Why Alexander Bell?' Clare at last asked.

'I saw men of my age disappear into their possessions. They became their cars, their stereos, their new apartments. They totalled their wealth and drank whisky late at night in smoky bars, looking sullen, looking sad. I wanted something else. It took me a long time to figure it out. I wanted a project to remind me of the complexity of things, and of human endeavour . . . does that sound pompous?'

'Not at all,' Clare said, leaning towards him.

'My uncle and I had begun exchanging confidences on

the phone and I began thinking, in almost boyishly simple terms, about what a marvellous invention this was. Wondering how it worked. When it entered the world. That sort of thing. I knew of Bell, of course, and his Scottish background may also have been an enticement, a kind of nostalgic attachment . . .'

Mr Sakamoto became momentarily shy. Clare smiled at him and nodded encouragement.

'And then,' he resumed, 'I realised there was something more here than the history of an invention. A man with a deaf mother and wife, who was obsessed with voice. Something anomalous. Endearing. Something beautifully particular. I suppose I fell in love with him: this burly fellow with a full beard and a life-long weakness for porridge . . .'

'I've seen the pictures,' Clare said, smiling. 'A love object, indeed.'

Alice felt they had begun talking in a kind of code. She wished she was not present at the dinner and began to think of when she might politely excuse herself, and leave them together.

'I discovered too that Alec Bell was permanently grief-stricken. A commonplace identification, I suppose, but he had lost two brothers and then two sons, and I felt this gave us a kinship, an emotional connection. Biography is always presumptuous, as friendship is.'

Here Mr Sakamoto glanced at Alice.

'But we function, do we not, on elective affinities, on the pertinent associations we find in others . . . ?'

'Well put,' said Clare.

'I've almost finished,' said Mr Sakamoto. 'Just a small section on Bell's visit to Japan in 1898, to meet the Emperor. I've been saving it until the end; it will be my conclusion. The Japanese connection, you might say.'

Clare drained another glass of wine. Alice thought she was

drinking too much. She had entered the slurry stage, her body tilted. A stage Stephen used to call 'imminent loss of verticality'. Alcohol was changing her, entering her metabolism like fog, obscuring the clear and distinct outlines of things.

'You lot are invading Edinburgh,' Clare suddenly announced.

Mr Sakamoto raised his head with a questioning look.

'You Japanese tourists. In hordes, every summer.'

Mr Sakamoto looked stricken. 'What is this collective noun I've become?' he said.

'Not you. The others.'

Alice could see Mr Sakamoto's dismay.

'It satisfies Westerners,' he said quietly, 'to see us as a collective, to make us uniform, to dishonour us in this way.'

Clare seemed not to be listening or not to understand.

'We are no less specific than you,' he went on.

'Westerners! Thanks very much.' Clare was leaning on the table. She tilted her glass.

'I was making an ethical point,' Mr Sakamoto said, 'about how generalisation destroys.'

They both fell silent. At some point in the dinner mild flirtation had dissolved and they were remade as antagonists.

'Don't be so touchy,' said Clare, with an aggressive tone.

Mr Sakamoto said nothing. Alice wondered if she had missed her chance to leave. If she left now, it might seem an act of punctuation to their dispute. Nevertheless, she rose, pushed back her chair, and said her farewells.

'It was nice meeting you, Clare. Enjoy the rest of your journey.'

Clare nodded vaguely in her direction.

'Phone me tomorrow,' Mr Sakamoto whispered, making once again the gesture of a phone shape with his thumb and curled hand. 'Tomorrow.'

Alice ran through the rain to the Métro station. The wet

streets were glazed with light, the air was chill and fresh. She felt the life of the city flare up around her. In its reflective multiplications, its rainy surfaces, it appeared streaming, bathed in a numinous glow. She was pleased to be away from the restaurant and in this bright liquid space. She felt youthful, released. The Seine churned with energy. Lovers were out and about, exhibitionist in their passion. Tilting their heads skyward to give and receive kisses.

*

It was almost noon by the time she rang. Mr Sakamoto was in his hotel room, packing to return home. Uncle Tadeo was unwell; he was leaving that afternoon. Alice was taken aback by this news: she couldn't imagine Mr Sakamoto leaving so soon, so abruptly.

'And Clare?'

'It got worse and worse. She ended up abusing me in language I'd heard her brothers use, years ago. Accused me of deserting her. We parted in acrimony. It was a terrible evening. She slipped and fell as we left the restaurant and when I bent down to assist her, she swore at me.'

'I'll come to the hotel,' Alice said. 'Come with you to the airport.'

Mr Sakamoto sounded pleased at the offer.

'Uncle Tadeo should have told me when he rang,' he said distractedly. 'I had to learn from Haruko that yesterday he rang me from a hospital bed.'

'What is it?'

'Some kind of flu. But it could be pneumonia. At his age, in any case, these things are far more serious.'

'Of course,' said Alice. 'I'm on my way.'

*

At the airport they drank coffee in an inhospitable café, ringing with noise. Chrome and aluminium clanged about them. A child was somewhere wailing. Mr Sakamoto appeared tired; his eyes were red from lack of sleep. A strange desolation passed over each of them. Alice reflected that this was yet another characteristic of airports – to induce generic dejection and slapdash conversation. But for Mr Sakamoto the cause was precise: he kept trying to ring Uncle Tadeo on his mobile phone, but got no response. They conferred on the reason. He may have been taken for tests; nurses may have confiscated his phone; perhaps he had switched it off in order to take a nap. There were a dozen reasonable explanations, Alice said. She tried to calm him, to mollify his alarm. Electronically modulated announcements, generated by machines, boomed into the café, incomprehensibly.

'Come and visit me,' said Mr Sakamoto, his voice gentle against the noise. 'How can you resist it? The kingdom of modernity, the empire of signs, gadgetry, robotics, futuristic inventions. You could meet my daughters. I could show you Nagasaki.'

Alice said 'yes' without even thinking. Yes, she would visit him in Nagasaki. Soon. Nagasaki.

She watched her friend enter the exclusive zone of scanning machines, metal detectors and antiterrorist devices. He passed under the archway that somehow knew if he was carrying a gun. He waved. Then he bowed. Alice also waved, and then bowed. The symmetry between them contested the turmoil all around, the rushing passengers, wheeling luggage, the airport staff, the rattling trolleys and impatient lines and bored mingling groups. It was a single event of neat correspondence. It was humane and tender. It was like theatre, like art.

*

In the city it was still light. Alice wandered the inner streets of Paris feeling bereft. Her time had been so governed by the presence of Mr Sakamoto — even on days when they met for only half an hour — that all was emptiness, now, and mere purposeless strolling. Shoppers carried plastic bags of groceries and clutched their baguettes; tourists peered into windows at Parisian delectables; elderly men and women strolled arm in arm. There were babies in prams, young people in trendy clothes, small dogs trotting along on extendable leads. There was a hum all about, the sound of daily life continuing, a sound congenial and easy on the ear. Stone, wood, concrete, metal: these held up the city before and around her with impressive solidity. She wondered what Paris-in-ruins would be like. What would this city be in a thousand years' time? What might remain? What might fall away? She moved as the traffic commanded, halted on the pavement by red lights, walked when given green permission. There might be decentralisation, no cities at all. There might be shattered spaces and underground retreats. There might be something from the movies: skyscrapers of vertiginous and impossible height, sky channels of zooming vehicles, never colliding, rocket-driven shoes and virtual windows in homes. Everything would be automated — food, sex. Everything would be subject to arcane systems of regulation and the haunting, invisible power of the state. Late capitalism. Simulation. New-improved forms of loneliness.

As Alice turned into rue Franc Bourgeois, she saw ahead of her, in the crowd, someone she recognised. It was not a friend, or a colleague, but a woman resembling herself. The woman had come out of a bakery holding a cardboard box tied with string, and as she stepped across the threshold from the store to the street, Alice saw her face in a three-quarter profile. It was an almost dreadful moment, a kind of teasing apparition, a joke, a mistake. Yet the resemblance was remarkable. The woman's hair was cut differently and a little longer, just past her shoulders, and she may have been slightly smaller in height, but overall the likeness was unmistakable. Alice began following the woman with the cardboard box, not sure exactly why, not sure what compulsion drove her. On the other hand, she reasoned, why wouldn't one follow one's chanced-upon double?

The woman with the box walked directly to rue Rivoli, then headed towards the Hôtel de Ville. The pavements were crowded with pedestrians, and once or twice Alice lost her, then saw again her bobbing head and firm trajectory. Alice was trying to decide if she should catch the stranger, and tap her on the shoulder, and surprise her in the way she herself had been surprised, but something inhibited her. Dusk was descending and perhaps this, above all, this sense of an indeterminate time of shadows and mauve air and the blinking on of sodium-vapour lamps, the time of ephemeral passage and uncertain presences, caused her to hesitate. She bumped into shoppers and workers hurrying home; she felt lumpish and slow. People's bodies were obstacles; their pale faces passed indifferently. This was, she supposed, closing-time clamour, the hurry towards exits and journeys home. All of a sudden the woman again disappeared. Alice accelerated a little, rushing forward, and realised that the woman had gone down the steps, into the Métro. Streams of people passed her, engrossed by destinations. Alice had paused only for a moment, but perhaps had lost her chance. She headed downwards into the concrete caverns, with their tunnels and signs and tiled routes into darkness, with their mechanical wind and tumultuous roar.

Alice had lost her. She should have been bolder and claimed the happy accident of resemblance. She walked back up the stairs, feeling her failure. And almost at once she began to doubt what she had seen: could she have simply imagined, or needed a mirror?

That night Alice dreamed of Mr Sakamoto. She was pushing through crowds, looking for someone. Figments and spectres swam in the air. People walked right through her: she was a nothing, empty space. Shop windows did not reflect her image. She descended steps and saw before her twin branching tunnels. Choosing the left, the more dimly lit (and thinking, in dream-thought: this is rather foolish), she came upon Mr Sakamoto waiting on an empty platform. He looked happy to see her. He smiled and opened his arms broadly in a welcoming gesture. His overcoat formed a shell; he became a refuge.

PART TWO

12

Tokyo from the sky.

Night navigation by aircraft, formally sheer terror, is one of the consummate art forms of the twenty-first century. Out of deep black, extending all the way to space, comes a pool of illumination, a nocturnal fire. It tilts and slides, as if insecure and unearthly, yet as the plane descends it begins slowly and by gradations to balance, becoming a disc, a shelf, a platform of arrival. At some thousands of metres one can detect concentrations of light and traceries of streets. One can look down upon systems, mysterious as any computer. There are logical patterns of identical shapes, mostly cuboid, rectangular, exceeding the boundary of the eye. There is a confusion of horizons and non-horizons, a fellowship of continuous spaces.

From her pod-like window, with her face pressed to the glass, Alice watched Japan come closer and closer. The plane dipped and circled. At a certain point she could make out billboards, vast and effulgent, coloured with a palette even Georges Claude would find astounding, and, beyond that, headlights of cars, the beaded tracks of highways and roads, the photosynthetic flare of shopping and commercial districts. *Electrical city.* This was Edison's dream. This was light in every form, dividing the shimmering world from the velvet darkness.

The plane landed with a thump, seeming to impress itself in the tarmac.

Alice stayed her first night in a hotel of crushing anonymity. The staff at the narrow front counter bowed and smiled, made intelligent signs to direct her to the elevators, but the 'businessman's choice' felt like a mausoleum. Lighting was dim and sombre; the corridors of the hotel, undecorated, had a fusty and airless atmosphere, and the room into which she gained access with her chunky key was a small brown box, dominated by an intrusive television mounted like a gigantic bug on the ceiling. There was a miniature shower cell, a telephone, and green plastic slippers wrapped in cellophane. The smell of stale cigarette smoke was all-pervasive. The windows would not open. The lamp was not strong enough to read by. It did not feel like Japan. It did not feel like anywhere. Outside, in a chasm seven floors below, traffic moved in restless queues, this way and that. From this distance the cars appeared wholly automatic, with no actual drivers or human component. Alice was reminded of funerals – their eerie systems of motorisation in removing dead bodies, their distended time.

A few weeks ago Mr Sakamoto had e-mailed, setting out the choices: the tourist hotel (which he recommended, but Alice decided she could not afford), the love hotel (strictly for liaisons; 'just in case,' Mr Sakamoto said), the businessman traveller's hotel (a.k.a. budget) and the sleeping capsule (the claustrophobe's nightmare). It had been a simple choice. She had booked on the internet, attracted by the fact the hotel was in the mellifluous-sounding Nishiogikubo district, and was the cheapest available on the list. Her disappointment was huge. Alice realised she had been entertaining in her head a kind of literary Japan – of screens and wooden floors and tastefully minimalist interior design. There was perhaps a *shackuhachi* flute playing somewhere in the distance and the sweet, tinkling sound of dripping water. Although she knew these items were unlikely to feature in a cheap Tokyo hotel, some part of her yearned irrationally for their reassuring appearance, for some indication, in any case, that was not this denuded hotel-land, blanked by corporate dullness.

Alice glanced around the room, her gaze coming to rest on the telephone. She would ring Mr Sakamoto tomorrow, when she arrived in Nagasaki.

Alice slept poorly and could not remember her dreams. In the middle of the night, her eyes flew open. Something, somewhere, had awoken her with a jolt. Outside the window was the whitish sheen of ambient neon light, and a billboard flashing, make-believing, speaking to everyone and no one.

*

Ground level. Daylight.

Tokyo was all verticality and titanium shine. Curved surfaces reflected people as jellyfish. There was fluted steel, trapezoidal glass and plasma-screen messages, escalators aplenty, virtual and actual realities. In the brown chemical haze, in the confusing thrum, Alice tried hard to orientate herself. She was helped at last by a myopic, crew-cutted stranger who directed her with hushed tones and butterfly gestures of the hand. When she could not understand, he helped her into a taxi.

The city was shifting its pixels, achieving and losing definition. Alice had a headache. A helicopter throbbed above, like a UFO. She closed her eyes, clutching her backpack, and summoned Mr Sakamoto's face, said hello to him, smiled and imagined him expressing delight at her arrival. Travel contained this instructive discombobulation. Alice was learning her foreignness, experiencing the *unbecoming* of places. Yet in her bafflement and travel-tiredness she was still exulted; the great city swung around her as the taxi pulled away. There was a frieze of colour, light, synthesised community. Glass towers bent above, replacing the sky.

The railway station was a booming labyrinth, stuffed with hurrying people. No one moved slowly. Fast motion was not, it seemed, exclusively cinematic; it was the quality that excited Tokyo citizens into post-modern haste. The crowd seemed to Alice good-looking, well-dressed and athletically speedy. Everyone but she knew where to go, and went there in a rush. She stood still, full of perplexity and admiration. There were signs she could not read – *kanji, katakana* – and glistening stalls of foodstuffs, trinkets and toys. Three stalls in her compass sold mobile phones: she was triangulated by their appeals and their handsome salesmen. One stall had as its emblem a cartoon phone with a smiley face and waving arms; it looked vaguely like a baby, as if phones were evolving nonsensically towards the human.

Almost at once a friendly stranger, a woman in her fifties dressed in a smart navy suit, stopped and asked Alice in English if she needed help finding her way. Alice gratefully agreed to be led to her platform. The woman expected no thanks, but bowed slightly and left quickly. Alice boarded the *shinkansen* to enter a super-woman-speed, to zip like a speeding bullet, on a power-ful locomotive, towards Mr Sakamoto, towards Nagasaki.

Could it be that one of the purposes of the invention of trains is to recover reverie? In the slide of landscapes and cityscapes there is a slide of consciousness, a drift, a pleasure of seamless conjugations. As Honshu flashed by, smudged by motion and the powdery light of industrial pollution, Alice entered the transport of her own random thoughts. The philosopher Henri Michaux once proposed the idea of a train-cinema. Along the route between Paris and Versailles, there would be placed a series of movable sculptures, activated by the speed of the train passing by. A superimposition and fusing of images would occur, so that the passenger would see outside the window a 'plastic' cinema, a spectacle of odd beauty and dislocated enchantment. Alice loved this idea. It seemed to her both thoroughly modern and to conjure the archeology of film – the turning of images, the persistence of vision. She settled back in her seat. It was deeply comfortable. The bullet train generated a hum, a kind of just-audible whisper of the friction of air. The passengers around her were asleep, or silently reading. They were all in altered states of being, all drifting somewhere. A child awake, a cute boy in a Yankees cap, stared out of the window, unblinking, as if hypnotised by a magician.

Alice was remembering a time with Stephen. When they were lovers she had often taken him with her to the movies. Like many philosophers, he began with an attitude of contempt, that this was a minor art form, an opium of the masses, sequences of facile and depthless distraction. 'Idiot art', he called it. Gradually, however, Stephen was won over. He forgot to resist and entered the spirit of images. Comedies, art cinema, even westerns – he learned to give himself fluently to screened experience. In the end they were almost undiscriminating. They went to film festivals, retrospectives, mass-release blockbusters.

It was in the middle of winter – they were both blunted by flu – when they went to see the 1964 Japanese classic *Woman of the Dunes*. The story was simple: an amateur entomologist from the city is looking for insects in a desert. There are montage shots of dune formations, grains of sand and scampering beetles. Having missed the bus back to the city, the entomologist, Jumpei, accepts hospitality from the locals. He enters a deep sand pit by a long rope ladder, and stays overnight with a woman in her ramshackle house. When Jumpei wakes in the morning he finds that the rope ladder has been removed, and that his hostess is outside, shovelling sand. He has been imprisoned as her 'helper'. The two are condemned to shovel sand so that they are not engulfed and buried. The other villagers lower water and supplies once a week to the woman and her unending labour is part of a peculiar natural economy – if her house is buried by sand, the other houses too will be lost. Sand leaks through the walls of the shack, it piles in pyramids at the doorstep, it falls in coarse grainy veils and sudden collapses. It has a ruthless incessancy. The man is overcome by anguish when he realises his entrapment. He looks up, but can see only a circle of sky and the taunting faces of the villagers, lined around the pit, waiting to haul up bags of sand. Jumpei must dig, or die. The woman says to him: 'Last year a storm swallowed up my husband and child. The sand came down like a waterfall.' This bleak announcement makes Jumpei frantic, but he cannot escape. Inevitably, the man and woman become lovers; there is a bathing scene of riveting eroticism. But overall the tone is hopeless. An indescribable melancholy envelopes the couple. At one point – a moment Alice found particularly affecting – the woman wishes for a radio, so that they might hear the world outside, so that they might know of a life beyond their deadly sand-trap. In the end there is no release, only the grim beauty of the black-and-white cinematography and the weird seduction of so stringent an allegory.

When they came home from the movie, Alice and Stephen made love. She kissed his chest as the Japanese woman kissed Jumpei, and tried not to think of the sand and the desert and the images that seemed so antisensual and unJapanese.

Stephen, too, she could tell, was in some halfway state of the imaginary, some dim zone between the screen and the body. He locked into her with a kind of desperation; he climaxed holding her fiercely, as if he were afraid of dying. Alice was a long time following, delayed by sand. Afterwards they lay side by side, both slightly feverish, both overtaken by the aftershocks of the movie they had seen. In low voices they spoke of it, and analysed its effects. Alice told Stephen about the cave-in in her father's mine, and his futile attempt to rescue his friends. She thought again and again of the phrase: 'The sand came down like a waterfall'. Stephen said that the movie was a poor attempt to represent Sisyphus. Eternal struggle, doomed effort, final meaninglessness. It scared him, he said. It was a damn scary movie. He had hated the bathing scene: 'the man was so passive', but he thought the actress wonderful.

Stephen fell asleep and later roused in a nightmare. He was making choking sounds and his arms flailed wildly, so that he accidentally struck Alice across the face.

'Help me!' he called out.

Alice switched on the bedside lamp. Stephen's eyes were open but he was still asleep. She touched his hot face and brushed back his hair. She leaned very close to his ear and whispered, 'It's all right, I'm here. I won't let you go.'

Stephen's eyes at last closed. His breathing eased. He slowly descended back into the territory of sleep and Alice was left behind, awake, staring into the black room that was refilling with images.

In the morning a bruise stretched across her cheek. Stephen did not recall any event in the night, so Alice told him that she had bumped into a door, stumbling, when she rose in the dark. She remembered her scarlet fever, and the hospital, and the nurse who had struck her. She remembered

James's distressed face and the radio broken on the floor, exposing its innards. She thought how curious it was that wounds by intention and accident look just the same. And how the special sadness of illness, its betokening objects, its loneliness, its timeless and fretful desolation, flow back into the present, unbidden, as a swoon before dawn.

*

Alice flicked through the notes she had brought with her on her travels. Among the articles and photocopies were several e-mails from Mr Sakamoto, who after departure from Paris had sent regular titbits on technologies and inventions. Since she had no phone, he said, he was obliged to e-mail. He apologised. He said too that he missed hearing her Australian voice. He missed their friendly conversations. Her answering smile.

Let me tell you, *he wrote*, about Magnetic Resonance Imaging, radio waves pulsing within the depths of the body.

The body is everywhere treated as mere surface: the cult of beauty, of youth, the existence of pornography – these are banal reductions, a fetish of surfaces. But the wise and the lunatic, the artist and the child, all know better. Under the skin is a noisy tumultuous space, muscles and organs and substances in concert, complicated goings-on and ingenious processes. Under the skin are the richest colours and a sweltering intensity. The anatomist carves flesh, the X-ray technician finds shadows, but MRI peers into the body without surgery or rays. Into the brain, into the viscera, into secret dark places.

Think of this: we are mostly water; we are two-thirds ocean. Because of our high water content the body can be exposed to a strong magnetic field and the molecules of our hydrogen atoms respond. When submitted to radio waves, the energy content of the nuclei changes and a resonance wave is emitted when the nuclei return to their previous state. Do you understand? Is this not the simplest of principles? Small differences in the oscillation of nuclei can be detected, so a three-dimensional image of the interior body can be built. The image shows the structure of the tissue, and reveals any pathology. Water, waves, magnetism, image: it is a kind of poetry. A physical *haiku*. Entering an MRI is like entering a radio coil; the radio waves cause the nuclei of the body to quiver and respond.

We are all thus collectors of waves, we are all creatures of hidden oceans.

*

The hotel room in Nagasaki was like the hotel room in Tokyo, except that it was smaller. Alice squeezed with her luggage through the door, which would not fully open because of the proximity of the bed, and saw before her an almost identical room – the brown walls, the suspended television, the green plastic slippers wrapped in cellophane. Outside the window was an electric Mitsubishi billboard, which she would discover alternated at night between Japanese and English script in white, orange and pink. The window opened. The hotel was near the railway station. Below her, straining her head out of the window, Alice saw a tram stop, with its arching tracks, what seemed like thousands of taxis, massed in waiting, and the monumental station itself, which incorporated a hotel, cinemas and a shopping centre. One façade of the shopping centre screened perpetual advertisements, like a colossal television, devoted to selling. It was early evening, still watery light, and pedestrians in restless movement filled the spaces between buildings, flowed over a footbridge, cinematically, to and from doors beneath the shiny screen.

Alice prepared to ring Mr Sakamoto. He had suggested she ring from Tokyo, so that he could meet her at Nagasaki station, and then take her home, but she had decided to surprise him, to ring 'out of the blue', with a gift-call for both of them.

A woman's voice answered the phone, speaking Japanese.

'*Moshi, moshi?*'

'May I speak', said Alice in English, 'to Mr Sakamoto?'

There was confused conversation at the other end. Someone was being called to the phone.

'Yes?' said another woman's voice, this time in English.

'May I speak to Mr Sakamoto? I am Alice Black, from Australia.'

There was a silence, then more background Japanese conversation. Alice thought at first she had rung the wrong number; she may have mistranscribed from the e-mail and lost her friend's details. But then the voice at the other end introduced herself as Haruko, Mr Sakamoto's daughter, and said that he was ill, and could not come to the phone.

'But I'm ringing', Alice insisted, 'from Nagasaki. I have come to visit. Your father invited me.'

Alice heard Japanese conversation once again and felt troubled by the evident alarm she had caused. There were tones of enquiry, of consternation.

Haruko's voice returned. 'My father is in hospital,' she said. 'We didn't know you were coming.'

Alice could hear an old man's voice, a thread she had not detected before.

'Our uncle', Haruko went on, 'says you must visit us tomorrow. I will pick you up, if it is convenient, for lunch. One o'clock? Please tell me your address.'

Alice was reeling. She read out her address from the hotel card.

'In the lobby, then. See you tomorrow.'

Alice heard a click and the voice was gone. She had not even had a chance to discover what was wrong with Mr Sakamoto, what hospital he was in, how she might reach him. There had been a tremor of anxiety in Haruko's voice by which Alice construed that her father's condition was serious.

Alice stared at the wall. It had been a foolish thing, not to tell Mr Sakamoto the date of her arrival. A girlish fancy. A trouble to everyone.

The room felt oppressive. Alice undressed and entered the small moulded shower cubicle. Under the warm water she closed her eyes. *The sand came down like a waterfall.*

When she was clean and had changed her clothes and dried her hair, Alice stepped into the streets of Nagasaki. They were lively, abundant. Streams of purposeful people parted before her as she walked, and her sense was of entering gusty circuits, all movement and energy. The shops were boxes of light, like television, and she was blown past them, randomly. There were clothes of remarkable elegance, stores of handbags, knick-knacks. Booths selling mobile phones were excessively visible. Alice saw again the baby-phone, with its bumptious smile. She headed away, into smaller, dimmer streets. In restaurants plates of plastic-modelled food ornamented the windows: Alice paused and looked closely at their garish forms. Parted *noren* curtains above doors, in the brightest indigo, waved customers in. She was hungry, she realised, but did not want to eat alone, conspicuously, in a restaurant. Alice wandered back to the area near the railway station and located a department store. When she entered, shop-girls in stiff uniforms bowed and greeted her with a sing-song chorus of '*Irashaimase! Irashaimase!*', and then she descended, like Orpheus, level after level, to the food hall she rightly surmised was below. There Alice bought a box of sushi, a capped glass tumbler of sake, and a French pastry sealed in a silver metallic wrap, all of which she took back with her to her hotel room. There, on the bed, beside the technicolour sign, she set out her simple meal and allowed herself at last to worry about her friend, Mr Sakamoto, somewhere else in this city, somewhere beyond the telephone.

*

She had been sleeping in awkward shapes. Her body ached when she woke.

In her rectangle of window Alice saw that the sky was overcast and drizzling, and that large birds, which looked like hawks, were circling above the railway station. The birds surprised her: she had seen their cousins in Australian deserts, but somehow here they appeared ominous and insidiously misplaced. Alice stood at the window, quietly looking down. Hundreds of umbrella shapes moved beneath her, grouping and ungrouping, forming designs, dispersing. Everything was oyster-coloured, dappled. The scene had a grave and unusual beauty. A print might be made of it. A modern-day Hokusai.

Alice dressed quickly and left the hotel in search of coffee. She was restive and disturbed. Not knowing Mr Sakamoto's condition had tilted her off balance. Alice drank two cups of strong coffee, then visited the Tourist Information Centre, which she had spotted in the same street as her hotel. She bought a tram pass and picked up pamphlets and a map of the city. She discovered she could visit Christian martyr sites and the Atomic Bomb Museum; she could go to the Peace Park or look at Western-style colonial houses or the reconstruction of an early Dutch settlement. It was still raining gently and the sky looked hazy. Alice returned instead to her hotel, to her small brown room. She lay on her bed, reading a novel by Murakami. Waiting like an impatient schoolgirl for lunchtime.

When Haruko met her in the lobby, Alice felt instantly relieved. She was dressed casually and had a relaxed and friendly manner; she seemed untroubled. Nothing serious, Alice told herself. Everything, after all, was going to be all right.

'Uncle Tadeo told us all about you,' she said, extending her hand. 'He knew you were coming, but wasn't sure when. My sister, Akiko, is at the hospital. She will join us later.'

'How is he?' asked Alice.

'I'm sorry I couldn't tell you on the phone. I had to look up the word in the dictionary. He has had what you call a stroke; he is blind and paralysed and will not recover.'

Alice simply stood. Haruko sounded brutally conclusive.

'But he was so healthy,' she said in a weak response.

'It happens, the doctor said. We were told not to hope.'

Told not to hope. Alice felt shocked and tearful. Haruko only now seemed to notice the measure of Alice's distress.

'Come to lunch, we will talk.'

'Can I visit him, then?'

'I'm sorry, only family.'

'How long . . . ?'

'About a week ago. He has declined since then.'

What did she see, in the wreckage of such shattering news? Mr Sakamoto's city from a watery car window, passing alongside her swiftly, like a ground-zero dream. Old-fashioned-looking trams, new-fashioned-looking shops, steep hills around the outskirts, holding up fragile-looking houses. A goddess statue, very erect, high up on a slope. A glimpse of the harbour, and slow, enormous ships. Haruko drove fast and was trying to point out sites of interest, but her heart wasn't in it. It was as if her practised cheerfulness had suddenly lapsed. They both fell silent for the second half of the journey. The rain grew heavier. Storm clouds in deep purple massed and gathered to the east.

Mr Sakamoto's house was in the traditional style; it was on a sheltered spur of the hillside and had survived the bombing, along with a small nearby cluster of other old wooden buildings. Rain darkened the wood. Alice and Haruko shared an umbrella from the car to the front door, and stood at the entrance, damp and dishevelled. Drips spattered in cherry blossom shapes on the floor.

Uncle Tadeo was there, awaiting Alice's arrival. He rose from his chair, bowed, and extended his arms widely, in a gesture of welcome. Alice was reminded of her dream of Mr Sakamoto in the Paris Métro. And although she was a stranger and had never seen him before – this wizened pale man, bald and frail and with the trace of a tremble – she walked into his embrace, rested her face on his chest, and began to weep. Uncle Tadeo touched Alice's hair and said something soothing. Haruko did not translate. It was not necessary. It was understood. Haruko too began to weep, and the three of them, together, were at once bonded in distress.

13

Akiko arrived at the family house soon after, looking strained and tired. She was wearing a heavy winter coat, which she did not remove. She said little to Alice, barely acknowledging her presence, and seemed to regard her as an intruder. Unlike Haruko, she was not confident in speaking English and settled as a silent, brooding presence. The small pattern of commiseration that Uncle Tadeo, Haruko and Alice had established was less stable in her company, and less able to be expressed. Alice apologised for her inability to speak Japanese: in this situation she felt blundering, reduced to clumsy gestures.

Haruko translated Uncle Tadeo's words.

'I was very sorry to hear about your bereavement.'

'Bereavement?' Alice felt that perhaps he had made an old man's slippage in time.

'Leo,' said Uncle Tadeo. 'Hiroshi told me about the death of Leo, and the flowers in the doorway, and your grief.'

Alice felt herself blush. It was three months ago. She hadn't even known him. She hadn't even spoken to him. What had Mr Sakamoto told his uncle?

'Thank you,' said Alice. 'He was young . . .' she heard herself add unnecessarily. Haruko somehow translated the hesitation to go on.

Uncle Tadeo spoke to his great-nieces in a way that Alice

realised was the tale of Leo. Uncle Tadeo's compassion was genuine and his concern complicated by the knowledge that his nephew was nearer than he to death. When he had finished his story, he looked up at Alice and nodded.

Alice asked again if she could see Mr Sakamoto, but was again denied.

'I'm sorry,' said Haruko. 'I've already asked. I rang the hospital this morning.'

So here she was, in Japan, with no Mr Sakamoto to talk to. Alice felt the huge weight of her redundancy and dislocation.

'You can stay with us,' said Haruko, as if reading her thoughts.

Akiko, in her large coat, shifted in discomfort.

'Thank you, but no,' Alice responded immediately. There was no question of her staying in his absence, no wish to see what might happen to the sisters, to Uncle Tadeo. No wish to make the situation more difficult.

'I'll return home,' she heard herself announce, even though she had not remembered making this decision. 'I've been gone from Australia for over six months. Perhaps it's time I saw my family.'

Haruko translated and Uncle Tadeo nodded sadly. Around the table, everyone was silent. They sipped green tea from delicate pink cups.

Outside a thunderstorm was booming above the house. Uncle Tadeo gestured to the ceiling with shrugged shoulders, and smiled wanly, as if asking forgiveness for the weather. Alice repeated his action. They liked each other. He was pleased she had come; he had wanted to meet her. He had heard daily accounts of the growth of her friendship with Hiroshi. Uncle Tadeo said something to Haruko and she rose from the table, left the room, and returned with a bulky manuscript, which she placed solemnly in Alice's hands.

'Uncle Tadeo thought you should see this. It's my father's book. *The Voices of Alexander Graham Bell*. He finished it only last month.'

Alice made a gesture of weighing it.

'Yes,' said Uncle Tadeo smiling. 'It's bigger than we all expected.' He was proud of his nephew. His eyes brimmed with tears.

It occurred to Alice that they were talking as if Mr Sakamoto was already dead. She was not prepared to relinquish him. She had not even begun to accommodate the news of his condition.

What would she do, without Mr Sakamoto?

After lunch Uncle Tadeo insisted they listen to a Beatles record. Haruko sorted through their record collection, retrieved *Abbey Road*, with its vaguely funereal cover, and put it on an old turntable that stood beside a new stereo system. Akiko left the room without saying a word and Uncle Tadeo fell almost immediately asleep. So Haruko and Alice were left together, hearing 'Come Together', 'Something', 'Maxwell's Silver Hammer', hearing the thunder and rain mingling with the historic tunes, which were playing from the past for a man who wasn't there. When they reached 'Octopus's Garden', both had had enough.

'Not one of my father's favourites,' Haruko said, as if giving herself an excuse to stop the play.

The music gave them no pleasure. It sounded sham, empty. The voices spilled into the room, and leaked away.

On the drive back to the hotel, Haruko explained that when their mother died, Akiko began to feel very cold. Nothing warmed her. Nothing at all. She kept her coat on all the time, even in bed. Now, she was responding to fear of her father's death in exactly the same way. Under cover. Retreating.

'She doesn't mean to be discourteous,' Haruko said. 'It's just her way. She is trying to cope.'

'Of course,' said Alice. She gazed out of the car window, watching the reversed version of her journey.

'"Yesterday",' Alice said.

'Yesterday?'

'It is one of his favourites. The song.'

'Ah,' said Haruko.

Her face was turned away. There was a complicity between them that adjusted and refined itself in these small exchanges. Rain-beat on the car roof soundtracked their pauses, made indirect intimacy possible, drew a film of wet silver over the too-sharp outlines of things.

Nagasaki was awash, shiny as cut opal in the drenching rains. A gem of light. The shuddering of fixed surfaces. Rain on the windshield distributed in fans.

What would she do, without Mr Sakamoto? What coat would she wear?

*

Adjectives, nouns, syntax, sequence: Japan was defeating Alice's sense of the intelligibility of things. She watched television, night-long, with the sound turned off, seeing in the glass chamber another kind of alphabet – of gestures, expressions, sincere on-camera communication, bodies touching, or staying apart, advertisements of demented eccentricity, showroom voluptuousness and bargain sparkle, dramas with faces twitching in exaggerated reactions, comedy, hilarity, clownish falling over.

When at last she killed the television, Alice lay on her back in the dark. Somewhere Mr Sakamoto was lying like this, festooned by tubes, linked to machines. As she was about to fall asleep, thinking of hospitals and images of the body, Alice recalled a long-ago photograph, Norah's X-ray photograph, that she had pinned for two years to her bedroom window.

When Norah was almost thirteen, she broke her right arm. It was encased in a heavy white plaster and she needed assistance with the simplest activities and actions. Alice was assigned to dress her, and to help her wash. Alice put on her shoes and socks, and tied her shoelaces. She plaited her sister's hair and added a ribbon. She helped carry her schoolbooks and wrote out dictated homework. At first both sisters were resentful and ill-tempered; Norah hated her dependency and Alice hated her servitude. But as the weeks passed — there were six in all — they entered a state of unprecedented intimacy: the everyday touching, the solicitude of the body, brought them eventually together, destroyed whatever unmentionable barrier had for so many years held them apart. This injury was the ground of their reconciliation. As Norah allowed her buttons to be done up she looked closely at Alice's face, concentrating on the task. She saw it, truly, for the very first time. Eyes, nose, cheeks, chin. Alice grew careful how she touched, and by degrees became as familiar with her sister's body as she was with her own. They both began to joke and to find the humour in the situation. They learned to talk to each other, and to be patient, to spend time looping in and out of each other's ideas, easy as swallows. At length, Alice and Norah found each other respectful. Sisterhood had taken this long to achieve.

At the window of Norah's bedroom hung her X-ray photograph. It showed her arm, an ivory lever, floating in a cloud of smoke. The fracture was clearly discernible. In the centre of the ulna was a long dark crack, almost half the length of the bone. Norah and Alice both thought the photograph wonderful. Against the window, translucent, it revealed the glossy frame of the inner body, the architecture beneath flesh, the taut structure of being. It hung like an icon. Both girls felt that they possessed a special knowledge. It healed them, bound them, signified bizarrely their belated coming together.

*

Alice dreamed that night that she was lost in a sandy desert that was Japan. She struggled through dense, impeding dunes, feeling her legs massively heavy and her heart heaving with effort. Her skin was encrusted all over with tiny grains of sand, her eyes were full of grit, her vision was blurred.

Ahead she saw, miraculously, the edge of a wheatfield. She hurried towards it and found Mr Sakamoto there, lying on his back, looking up at the sky. All around rustled the desiccated stalks of wheat. They made a soothing sound, like the sound of falling rain. Mr Sakamoto did not seem to recognise her. He lay perfectly still, his arms outstretched in cruciform. Occasionally he blinked. He looked calm, composed.

Alice saw the blue sky reflected in his eyes. It looked like water. It looked to Alice like Mr Sakamoto was filling up with water.

And then, in the distance, Leo appeared. He wore earphones and was mutely nodding to his music, swaying a little, tapping his sneakered feet. Alice wondered in dream-land if he was dead or alive, if he had reached a drop-zone somewhere, of limbo, or perdition, or if this dumb show to futile, unprotecting sound was the condition, after all, of every soul: something is missing, something is always missing.

*

On her second morning in Nagasaki Alice felt even more lost. She woke early, carrying into consciousness her disturbing dreams, but felt unmotivated, inert and exhausted. She could not bear to remain here, waiting in a morbid vigil for Mr Sakamoto to die. She would change her airline ticket immediately and tell Haruko and Uncle Tadeo. Perhaps she would return to Japan another time. Akiko would be pleased to see her go. She had enough to deal with, without unwelcome visitors. Alice was haunted by the shape of her, crouching miserably in her overcoat, hunched like a survivor of war, like a refugee. A single death could do that: reshape an existence.

The rain had ceased but the sky was still overcast and gloomy. Hawks – or something like them – continued to wheel above the station. Alice had a dinner appointment with Haruko, but otherwise was free. Yet she felt unlike a tourist, more like an interloper. If she had been able to see him, she thought, she would be at rest; she would be able to encourage him to live, perform a miracle, or say goodbye. She would at least know what he looked like and how he was suffering. She would take bright flowers. She would kiss his forehead. She would speak to him in a low voice, there, at the bedside, tangled with tubes and medical machinery.

As it was, Alice stood in the hotel room looking down at the city, feeling as if someone had torn at her insides. She would try to read. Reading was a fissure she could fall into, a warm space with two walls, a sweet forgetfulness. She rocked on her heels, scanning for meaning. City-buzz streamed upwards carrying human and non-human sounds, the hot-wire rumble of alert machines, the cellphone chatter of a million telepresences.

*

'I went nowhere,' Alice confessed. 'Nowhere at all. I stayed in my hotel room and read a novel.'

Haruko looked concerned. She offered to take her guest sightseeing, but Alice refused.

'I will go to the Atomic Bomb Museum, perhaps tomorrow, because I feel I must. But otherwise, I will leave. This feels all wrong, Haruko. I have no wish to enjoy myself with him lying there . . .' She could not say the word 'dying'. Alice was having trouble containing her feelings. Haruko, however, appeared composed and wise. She seemed in manner very like her father. She wore a tan dress of raw silk and a tailored brown jacket. Alice felt shabby beside her and without emotional poise.

'I'm sure you will return,' Haruko said kindly, 'in other circumstances.'

They were in the small private booth of a noisy restaurant. At intervals, unintrusive women in rustly kimonos slid aside their paper screen. They brought artfully constructed dishes, each small and compactly designed, on black laquered trays. Fish, rice, mushrooms, pickles. Alice wondered how Mr Sakamoto had been able to enjoy heavy French food served with a clunk on gigantic plates. She liked the fastidiousness of chopsticks and the sundry range of dishes. The slow processing through the meal. The frills, the flourishes, the garnishes that were pink and green and stacked as chrysanthemums or pagodas.

'It is something', Alice said, 'your father and I share. A love of food. We had many meals together.'

'He told me,' said Haruko. 'He once rang and said he had met a woman who talked as he did and was interested in food. You had just been out to the movies together. We thought he was falling in love. It was a shock to learn your age.'

Alice paused. 'It's a friendship,' she said carefully.

Haruko smiled. 'I know. Don't worry. Uncle Tadeo was fascinated and he interrogated my father. We know all about you.'

Here Haruko smiled again. Alice felt uneasy.

'You've heard, perhaps, of their special relationship — my

father and Uncle Tadeo. It's rare between men, I think. They know each other's secrets. They tell their lives and thoughts in detail. They even tell each other their dreams. This time is hard on my Uncle Tadeo. He is missing the telephone calls. He is missing Hiroshi's voice.' Haruko fell silent. 'It's hard on all of us,' she added.

After a few cups of warm sake, Alice and Haruko both began to relax. The noise in the restaurant was growing louder, but they seemed enclosed in a room of relative quiet. Alice wanted to say: *I know things about you too*, but instead, searching for a neutral bridge of words between them, she asked Haruko about the *kamishibai* man.

'Ah, I suppose he said Akiko and I adored the *kamishibai* man. In truth he was the one who always suggested the visits. We wanted to watch television. My father has an affection for storytelling and redundant technologies. We used to go to the library with him and watch the *kamishibai* man perform. He was a man in his seventies, I suppose, and his equipment – the *hyoshigi*, the wooden clappers used to start the performance, the little stage he showed his pictures on – these were probably from the 1920s. But he was agile and gifted, especially with accents. We always resisted going, but when the story began we were always entranced. There was a particular folk tale we loved, "The Bamboo Princess".'

'Your father mentioned it,' Alice said. 'He told me the plot.'

Haruko looked up from her bowl of *agadashi tofu*.

'My father hated the idea that the Bamboo Princess left her parents, so he made up his own endings. Did he tell you that?'

Alice shook her head.

'In my father's version, the Bamboo Princess takes her parents with her to live on the moon. No parent, he used to say, would exchange the elixir of life for separation. So there is a little family up there, never separated. Over time he added bits and pieces to the story. The Bamboo Princess recovered brothers and sisters she thought she had lost; she met a Bamboo Prince, with a similar history of exile. They fell in love, of course, and were married under earthrise. He used to sit between our beds as we were falling asleep and tell and retell 'The Bamboo Princess', adding each time a fresh detail to the story, a twist, an adornment . . . I actually believed she was up there, up in the moon. Sometimes, as a small girl, I talked to her. But I really didn't believe my father's happy family version. And I suppose I rather liked the idea that she had a space to herself, that she had deliberately chosen it, that she was at home, and remote.'

'I was always told,' said Alice, 'that there was a man in the moon.' She heard herself sounding trivial. She felt dull, boring.

'No, no, not at all. You can see her face. She has a round Japanese face, pale as a geisha.'

Haruko laughed and leaned back from the table. Alice noticed her slender hands around the square wooden sake bowl. She wore no rings, no jewellery of any kind.

'How did you meet my father?'

'Uncle Tadeo didn't tell you?' Alice asked wryly. 'We were on a train, between Chartres and Paris. An old-style train. One that rocks, that stops frequently, is rattly and slow. Someone played John Lennon's 'Instant Karma' and we began talking. I liked him at once, his candour, his humour. Then we discovered we were both, in a sense, researching technology – he with his biography of Alexander Bell, I with a book on the poetics of modernity. He seemed to take for granted the idea that my project was worth pursuing. It gave me confidence. Our friendship consists almost entirely of shared meals and long talks. Talks about anything.'

'Did he talk of my mother?' Haruko asked.

'Not very much.'

Alice told her the story of the Spanish astronaut and the abbreviated honeymoon. Of his sense of despair.

Haruko looked down at the table. 'It always seemed such an estranged marriage to me. I never understood how they got together.'

The screen slid open and a waitress came in to remove more dishes. Haruko spoke to her rapidly. Alice was feeling drunk and hoped she was not ordering more sake.

'Green tea,' Haruko said, when the panel closed. 'Otherwise neither of us will be able to walk out of the building.'

Alice smiled at her and said nothing. She was again reading thoughts.

'Do you want company at the museum tomorrow?'

'No,' said Alice firmly. 'But I would like to say goodbye to Uncle Tadeo. Can I call on him sometime in the afternoon? I'll catch a taxi.'

It was settled. Over whisked green tea in Hagi china bowls, they made a plan for Alice's last day in Nagasaki. She felt the mixture of euphoria and despondency that drunkenness induces. Alice had spent her day in words, evading the real; now the physical world asserted its substance and irreducibility. When she stood up from the low table she misjudged the space and banged her knees, then as she caught herself toppling she knocked over a bowl. Haruko leaned forward across the table and held her elbow. The panel door opened, yet again, and a sash of orange light illuminated Haruko's blouse. Everything was vague and receding. Haruko said something to the waitress and a pair of hands reached under Alice's armpits and helped her from the cavity beneath the low table. She was embarrassed, and at a loss. She felt metaphysically uncoordinated. Huge kimono sleeves embraced her and almost carried her from the restaurant. There was an embroidered crane visible through her alcoholic haze. A decoration, perhaps, an unexpected vision of something illogically beautiful.

*

On the tram Alice counted the stops so that she would not miss the museum. She was standing up, crushed within a group of secondary school students, who talked across her, giggled, sent and received text messages on their mobile phones. The school uniform was dark blue, prim and formal, modified by the girls with hitched-up skirts and socks with lace trimming. Boys had loosened their ties and mussed their hair and looked a little rakish. Every school bag bore fluffy or plastic accessories. Alice was pleased to be travelling like this, in the embrace of this youthful exuberance. She felt she understood them. If she spoke Japanese she would strike up a casual conversation, discussing television or movies. As it was, standing so very close to their faces, she thought how attractive they appeared, their hair, their black eyes.

Alice found her stop and followed the signs up a steep street to the white museum building. Wet blossoms lay in the gutter and blew alongside her. She expected crowds at the museum, but there were none. It may have been too early in the day, or perhaps this was not a popular site. The foyer to the museum appeared almost empty – one of those ringing public spaces, perpetually clean – but for a display against one wall of objects and illustrations made of origami paper cranes. There were strings of cranes in every colour, cascading in a kind of waterfall, forming peace signs and peace objects, collage-created images of doves and flowers. School children from across the world sent origami cranes to this place.

Alice was thinking: I'll be OK; I can cope with the A-Bomb Museum.

But then she truly entered. The architecture of the

building was such that one walked down a spiralling ramp, descending from light and cranes into the dim area of exhibition. The walk in downward spirals was disconcerting and Alice felt a sense of dread. It was like walking into a pit, like moving slowly underground. There was a muffled hush and a sense of overheated enclosure.

At the bottom she entered shadowy corridors and sombre spaces. Near the entrance to the exhibition, almost in darkness, was an exploded wall clock, halted at 11.02 on 9 August 1945. Opposite were six large video screens, playing and replaying, in a continuous loop, six mushroom clouds photographed from B29 bombers. They rose in a grainy, scratchy slow motion. They were quiet, compellingly abstract, yet also carried the routine associations of black-and-white film – old news reels, war movies, the smell of cigarette smoke. Six mushroom clouds were five too many: someone, perhaps the curator, imagined multiplication would register unthinkable dimensions. The bonfire of humans. The ghastly thunder.

A group of school children, no older than ten, hurried past Alice and moved on, chattering ahead of her. She could hear them exclaiming. There was an echo effect here, a distortion of sound. Alice turned a corner, following the children's voices. Objects and images of catastrophe rose to meet her. She could barely look. A steel helmet with the wearer's skull fused to the inside, hand bones embedded in melted glass, a schoolgirl's charred lunchbox, tatters of clothes, any number of mournful, forfeited things. There were photographs of grievous burns and women cradling dead babies, survivors with no skin, people reduced to effigy. Photographs of blasted space, all mud and ash. A smouldering primary school, a shattered cathedral, a whole town gone. Everywhere Alice looked there were lists and statistics: deaths – 73,884; injuries – 74,909. The names of schools and their numbers of students, of patients in hospitals, workers in factories, inmates in prisons. Children's high-pitched talk threaded the gruesome numbers and images. Two girls murmured nervously before a description of the effects of gamma rays and radiation. Alice wondered why they were allowed here – so young – to see all this. All this atrocity and ruin. All this documented death, shrill with agonies.

Alice tasted mud in her mouth. She felt a constriction in her chest and moved towards the exit. There, as if to capture her, were witness testimonials, with English language translations. Alice glanced at the words and could not stop herself from reading. Accounts from children, young adults. A British prisoner of war. A Buddhist monk. The narratives seized her almost as if they were overheard utterance, whispered for her alone, directly into her ear.

From the window I saw my mother in the garden, picking aubergines for our lunch. She burst into flames.

Voices told of bluish light, then unforgettable fire. Of skin burst open, and tempura oil used as medicine. Of shoes stuck to melted asphalt, the soles of feet burning. Of defoliated trees, of featherless birds raining from the sky.

Alice fled the museum, spiralling upwards. Time shuddered and stopped. Heaviness of being. Death clouds. Ash. She found herself back at the tram stop without remembering anything of her walk there. She felt numb, vacant, caught in a dismal trance. Then the material *now* intercepted: here was the tram, here it came, to carry her physically away. Alice boarded the tram, rode shakily, and almost missed her stop at the railway station. When she disembarked she walked quickly through the crowds to her small brown room. There she could sit still, alone and in silence. Alone. In silence.

*

Akiko had not been present, but Alice, Haruko and Uncle Tadeo had spent a surprisingly pleasant afternoon together. Uncle Tadeo proudly showed Alice their raked stone garden, pointing out to her the sinuous consistent curves around a central shape, the pond with a bamboo drip, a stone resembling a mini-mountain, a granite lantern.

'Your nephew', said Alice, 'says the raked garden is a picture of sound waves.'

Uncle Tadeo nodded. 'It is,' he confirmed, pleased that she knew. He made witty remarks and asked curious questions about Australia. Haruko patiently translated. Then she talked to Alice about her job, and her love of literature. Over tea she seized Alice's hands and made her promise to return.

'I promise,' Alice said. There was no question, somehow. She knew it to be true.

Uncle Tadeo smiled.

Alice left before dinner, claiming she was tired, with parcels of gifts and sincere embraces. To Uncle Tadeo Alice had given a small Aboriginal wood carving of a kangaroo, intended for Mr Sakamoto. It was a charming object, rough-hewn, the colour of desert. Uncle Tadeo bowed and tucked it in the front of his *yukata* robe, making a joke about pouches. When she was leaving, his eyes filled with tears. Haruko would not hear of Alice catching a taxi, and drove her back to the centre of the city.

'I will stay in touch,' said Haruko. 'I will let you know what happens.'

Alice visited the department store and again bought sake and sushi, and ate once more on her bed in the hotel room. She fell asleep very early. She would pack in the morning. She would catch the 10.30 train directly to Fukuoka, then switch to the *shinkansen* for the route to Tokyo.

Alice woke with a start in the middle of the night, thinking of herself, obscurely, as a silhouette. Visits to museums always resulted in this accumulation of images, this messy spilling over. But when she was fully awake, she realised she was thinking of Mr Sakamoto. The silhouette was a child. A small boy, running, his legs flying up behind him. Alice tried to imagine what Hiroshi Sakamoto, as an eleven-year-old boy, had witnessed on that cloudy August morning. His house had been on a south-east ridge, protected from the blast. Had he run down the hill, looking for his sisters, for his father, for his tutor, Harold O'Toole? What had he seen before him? Had his feet burned on melted asphalt? Were there bodies all around? Was the sky like a shroud?

The electric billboard flashed in on Alice's imaginings. She was a stranger here, she knew nothing, she could only guess. She could not enter into Mr Sakamoto's experience. She rose from her bed and switched on the light, and, having nothing better to do, began her meagre packing. An image from the museum surfaced inside her. It was a photograph of the shadow of a man and a ladder, imprinted by the blast on a wall. A persisting shadow. That was all. An autograph of death.

14

In clear light, flights over Australia showed the continent as a crimson body. You could almost believe it was skin there, mottled, veined, incised with scarification, tattooed with blue print, bulging, recessed. Cloud shadow accentuated these incarnations. Curves arose, a suggestive crevice, the flank of a ridge resting seductively, like an arm on a pillow. Other countries appeared, more inhumanly, in green or grey, and Alice had forgotten this fleshly appeal, this summoning of matters of skin, of sex, of appetite. It was good to return. To skim across the river. To sit with her legs in the sun. To hear raucous birdcall in a cobalt sky.

At the airport everyone seemed to dial on a mobile phone as soon as they left the plane. Such frail cargo. There was an urgency in saying *yes,* we have arrived safely from the sky; we have managed to journey from the other side of the planet. Travellers who had been in sedated suspension and dull disengagement, now spoke in loud, unnatural voices. There was a kind of pleasure in the air, a tremble of call and responsiveness. Conversations of all kinds were developing, overlapping and warm tones everywhere met with other warm tones. Alice remembered something Mr Sakamoto had once told her about Alexander Graham Bell. Alec was fascinated, Mr Sakamoto said, by the phenomena of 'sympathetic vibration'.

Playing the family piano, he discovered that by pressing the pedal that lifted the felt dampers from the piano wires, then singing into the piano, he could sound the wire that matched the pitch of his voice, the others remaining silent. He also discovered that one piano would echo a chord struck on another one nearby. This inspired Alec to try to invent an 'electric piano', by moving electromagnets beneath each wire. But he returned, in the end, to the simplicity of agile fingers dancing over ivory, and the press of a single foot on a shiny brass pedal. 'He returned to the body,' Mr Sakamoto had said firmly.

Alice was thinking of sympathetic vibration when she saw her sister in the crowd. In the history of families there exist moments of raw shock, when one exposes oneself, or sees exposure, or links in some private way to a self normally hidden. The shock was in realising that Norah had not revealed her illness, but had entered the valley of the shadow of death and suffered there, and struggled, without telling her sister. One breast had been removed, and now she was fixed into regimes of drugs and chemotherapy. When Norah met her at the airport she had been out of hospital for only three weeks. Her skull was exposed and her body blue and emaciated. Alice embraced her sister and Norah returned the embrace fiercely, as if she was drowning. They looked into each other's faces.

'Why didn't you tell me?' Alice asked. 'Why?'

But Norah could not answer. She turned away.

Michael, who was standing nearby, said 'Righteo, then,' and Alice realised she had not acknowledged her brother-in-law. They offered each other perfunctory hugs. Michael looked uneasy, abashed. He reached forward to take Alice's case.

'The kids are with Mum and Dad,' Norah announced. 'We'll head there together. They're all dying to see you.'

Alice linked her arm with her sister's while Michael carried the luggage. Norah felt hot, mortal. She was so thin Alice could feel the form of her bones beneath her skin; it was as if she were holding someone breakable. Alice grasped her protectively. The airport terminal was full of people, all with trolleys or wheeled cases, rattling along, avoiding collisions. So much clattering. Alice heard the greetings on arrival, the unexpected surprises, the embraces, the questions. Then Michael's mobile phone rang, playing the *Star Wars* theme. He stopped and released the luggage while he snapped open his phone and answered the call. Norah and Alice stood waiting, bound together by great, unsayable things, by the sympathetic answering of one to another, like pianos communing.

*

Her apartment had a musty, closed-up smell. Alice drew the curtains, opened the windows and looked around at her books, her table, the souvenirs of her travels. Items in the room asserted their claim on her: she was this, she was that, she had been to India, to Spain. She was someone who read way too many books. The television looked enormous – a bulb of glass, waiting. The radio was there, the CD player, the simple black reading lamp she had always loved. The stillness was reassuring; everything was in its place. As Alice looked at the telephone, it began suddenly to ring. It rang and rang, but she did not pick up the receiver. She realised she was expecting the answering machine to click on, but she had disconnected it, months ago. The more she waited the louder and more insistent the calls seemed to become. It may have been Haruko, she thought after a few seconds.

'Yes?'

'I knew you were there, hiding. Norah told me when you were coming back.'

It was Stephen. Oh no, Alice thought. Oh no.

'I'm ringing to invite you to dinner. To meet my new girl-friend. It would mean a lot to both of us.'

Alice was exasperated and tired beyond patience. She could barely bring herself to respond.

'I've just got back from the airport, Stephen. Can we talk later?'

'It's just that we really need to make a time and place.'

Alice knew there was no shaking him.

'Next Friday at eight. At Benito's.'

Alice put the receiver down without saying goodbye, just as he had not said hello. She felt foolish, agreeing so readily to see him. He had caught her off guard. He would demand things, bring his pathos with him in a bundle on his back. She pulled the phone lead from the wall. Haruko, surely, would not ring this soon.

*

The summer weather had begun and the days were long and bright. Alice was woken by loud birds, squabbling and feeding in the bushes and trees near her apartment. Magpies called to each other with sovereign command. Wattle-eaters cackled. There were kookaburras far off, in the stand of tall salmon gums down near the river and the brash distant caw of a flock of black cockatoos. Here, at home, she could identify the birds.

Alice rose, pulled on jeans and a T-shirt, ate a small meal of fruit and headed for the river. Often she would simply walk its banks, grateful for the enlarged sky, the return of colour to the world, clean wind from the coast sweeping into her lungs. In her jet lag the world was susceptible to fractures and elisions. Sometimes time slowed, and her body remembered the northern hemisphere, its sluggish inclinations; sometimes it accelerated, so that she lost an entire hour. She had flown from Tokyo to Paris and then back to Australia. Her zigzag around the planet had left her slightly crazed, cracked in what she imagined was the globe of her self. Five days had passed since she left Tokyo and she had not heard from Haruko. Five days.

Alice lay on her sofa listening to music. Bob Dylan, The Smiths, Tom Waits, Nick Cave: all of it world-weary and moaning, sad men in dark crumpled jackets, their eyes lightly closed, tilting silver microphones into smoky half-light. She played 'A Hard Rain's A-Gonna Fall' to hear the line about a dozen dead oceans, and she remembered Leo, and the allure of solitary music.

What Alice could not understand was Norah's secrecy. Her sister had been able to write of the Iraq war and to chat about home life, but was unable to disclose her own serious news. Illness had severed them, when it should have brought her home. Perhaps she had not yet warranted or earned Norah's trust; or perhaps the husband and family had erased those dependencies, those secrets the sisters might want to keep together. An old longing resurfaced, to have Norah's approval. Old as the day, years ago, of the slaughtered kangaroo, when the gore of it and the muck of it and the skull-cracking violence had slanted her family's feelings complexly against her, had weakened something simple that might have been shared between them.

In the drear space of waiting, of slow elapse, Alice was unsure of how to spend her time. She tried to read the newspapers, but found herself sickened. War, refugees. Asylum seekers in Australia held in cruel detention. She was succumbing to the havoc of her many emotional misalignments. The country felt physically the same, but otherwise depressed her. History had given them this: the wounded and dispossessed held behind razor wire, contiguous, somehow, with green tracer lights at night preceding explosions, nineteen-year-old soldiers shooting nervously in the dark, tanks, bombers, missiles, grenades. Television collapsed distance: loss and war was everywhere, filling up eyeballs all over the planet. There was no limit, it seemed, to what might be shown, what thinnest apparitions might come to haunt you, what remote event, what fucked-up invasion, might veer into assaulting, hideous proximity. On the sofa, unrelaxed, Alice felt overwhelmed. She was waiting for whatever would trigger a release. If Mr Sakamoto had been with her, she would have found something to marvel at; she would have been reminded of the other side of things, which rests beyond shadows.

*

Alice arrived at the restaurant a little late. In the Australian style, it was decorated with dead sticks, jutting at inorganic angles from the ceiling, and uranium-yellow walls, streaked with fake rust. Stephen was talkative and keen to impress. He introduced his girlfriend, Karen, who was pretty and quiet, and worked, she said, as a kindergarten teacher. She had long blonde hair, which she twirled in her fingertips and seemed unable to leave alone. Her distracted fidgeting kept catching Alice's attention, sometimes mid-sentence, so that she heard herself halting in speech and becoming self-conscious, wondering how this woman had retained such childish habits. The restaurant was full and noisy, brittle with the sounds of crockery and laughter. They made small talk and Alice felt the return of jet-lagged exhaustion. She looked at her hand clutching a napkin and thought of Mr Sakamoto.

And then, at no particular moment, Stephen leaned forward, earnestly. 'I have an announcement,' he said. 'I'm going to be a father.'

He took Karen's hand and she smiled shyly. Someone dropped what sounded like a tray of cutlery. The air rang with spoons, forks, clashing knives. In the midst of this commotion, Alice disguised her surprise and congratulated them both. She leaned across the plates and gave each a kiss on the cheek.

'I'll have a family, Al. I'll make a real go of it.'

He spoke in an overloud voice to defeat the noises from the kitchen. Stephen had not called her Al since they were at university together. Alice looked across at Karen, who was staring at her plate, and felt a flood of tenderness for them both.

'You'll make a wonderful father, Stephen. And I'm sure you, Karen, will be a wonderful mother. With all your experience with children.'

It was a simple gesture of goodwill, but it was what the couple had waited for. Both, for some reason, wanted her approval. Alice wondered what Stephen had told Karen of their relationship. What authority he had given her. She proposed a toast, 'To new families'. They echoed the words, 'To new families', holding their smudged half-empty wineglasses towards her. Stephen smiled widely. Alice could not recall, for years, seeing him so happy.

It was perhaps a kind of residual possessiveness, perhaps a kind of sexual nostalgia, but Alice remembered his face on a pillow, long ago, laughing, his head resting in the crook of his arm. She was relieved at his news, truly relieved, and saw in that moment of announcement the glimpse of a man who was self-possessed and newly open to joy. What women learn of men in bed is more than they can imagine. Their modes of assertion and retreat, their forms of pride and shame, their capacity for pleasure, longing, for the sweet wing-spread of desire. What they might say, what story . . . Alice roused from her passivity and thought: this is a true celebration. And as she drove home, carefully, along the highway lined with sodium vapour lights and signs in neon, lights which extinguished the stars, which mapped the city in flagrant stripes against the soft curve of the river, she felt too, more than anything, a kind of emancipation.

*

Because Stephen had asked her to, Alice visited his mother, Margaret, in hospital. She had no wish to enter a hospital. Not now, preoccupied with Mr Sakamoto, connected sympathetically in the time of his dying, and the waiting, and the sad wish that it would soon be all over. But maybe, she thought perversely, she could visit Mr Sakamoto by visiting Margaret. Not as a substitution, but as a kind of veneration, a tribute to the expectation of loss.

The oncology ward was for some reason painted grey. Hospitals demanded the surrender of even the barest forms of indulgence. Alice made her way through halls and along labyrinthine corridors that echoed with unseen footfall and the intimation of sharp metal instruments. There were huge lights above, like monster eyes, and the floors were polished to a high, treacherous shine. Alice felt she was sliding, as nurses sometimes appear to do. As one might in a dream. She wondered if this was where Norah had stayed, in this very place. If she had been diagnosed here. Had her operation here. Rested alone, hemmed in by high grey walls. Suffered anguish. Solitude. Alice was ashamed of how little she knew. She must ask Norah. She must recover the lost story. Perhaps she was not here, after all, for Mr Sakamoto, but in expiation for her unintended neglect of her sister. She did not know Stephen's mother well: they had met only a few times, when mother and son had briefly reconciled during his time at university.

Margaret shared her room with three elderly ladies, all in conditions of dire ill health. She was reading when Alice entered, and looked up from her book, holding her place in the text with her index finger. She smiled.

196

'Hello, stranger,' she said, turning the corner of her page. 'Stephen phoned to say he'd seen you and that you were coming in. But I really didn't expect you to visit so soon.'

Stephen should have warned her: his mother was almost unrecognisable. She too was a stranger.

Margaret's face was caved and her skin was semi-transparent, so that the veins were apparent, the contours, the inner face. Filaments of hair flew up from the top of her skull. Alice leaned forward to kiss her and found that her cheek felt like paper. Margaret had a tube inserted in her arm and another leading somewhere under the sheet. Behind her rested a box, blinking with an electrostatic glow. She shifted position and patted the bed, indicating that Alice should sit.

'Here, now,' she said.

Here, now. For Alice the words were both overloaded and hypothetical. *Here, now. Nuance and eternity* – everything intersected in these places of despair. Words were mutating, volatile with new meanings. She sat on the edge of the bed, wondering what she would say.

'How about it, eh?' Margaret said. 'Stephen and Karen.'

'They're a lovely couple. And Stephen seems so happy.'

'I intend to stay around to meet my grandchild.'

'Good for you,' said Alice.

They talked of everything but her illness. They talked mostly of times past, and Alice explained why she had not stayed with Stephen. Margaret began to reminisce.

'I don't regret leaving my marriage, but it was hard on Stephen. I should have taken him with me, but I felt a nothing, a nonentity. I felt completely inadequate. Living with Bill had worn me out. When he was drunk Stephen and I would haul him onto the couch, then we'd sit in silence at the kitchen table, drinking cups of tea. We never really knew how to console each other. When Bill started at the whale yards it all became harder. When he touched me I felt contaminated. I could smell the stink of blood and guts on his skin. I hated the thought of all that butchering. All day, cutting up an animal, knee-deep in flesh. I remember thinking: I married a fiddler, a handsome man dancing a jig, and now he spends his days in a slaughterhouse and carries death into the home. For months I thought about it, then one day I just left. I wrote to Stephen often, but he never replied. Only now, only recently, we've really started to talk. Started to know one another. I think he's scared that I'm going to die, but I'm a tough old biddy, I tell him. I'll go on for ever. And now Karen. And the baby . . . I always thought it would be you. That you'd be the one.'

When Alice left, she felt that it had been a good visit. Margaret had been pleased to see her and they had talked frankly, and with trust. They had found under the monster lights and the medical machines a few clear honest words.

'Come again,' Margaret said.

A sliding nurse had come to take her blood pressure and Alice was being sent out the door. She looked back at Margaret, palely loitering, but was again thinking about Norah, her bony body, her diminishment, her teetering-near-death.

*

In the days that followed, the waiting days, Alice spent time with her family. Fred had aged in her absence, but Pat looked just the same. Her father walked with a kind of shuffle, his maroon slippers scraping unevenly at the carpet, and seemed rather bent, at an angle to the world. They sat on the couch together, watching video-taped football matches, and Pat entered and left, bringing tea and biscuits on a tray. It was their usual ritual. It was the pattern into which she and her parents fitted so that they knew how to be together. Alice and her mother washed and dried dishes, standing side by side. She raked leaves in their garden and helped Pat with the crossword puzzle in the newspaper. She carried bags of shopping. She arranged a vase of yellow roses they had chosen together from a roadside stall. Casual, quiet actions were their cohesion, their love.

At Norah's house, Alice played with her niece and nephew, lying on the floor among a scattering of plastic toys. They climbed on her body and treated her as furniture. It was wholly delightful. Helen and David had grown quickly and were little individuals now, each particular in their habits and tastes, and each competing for her attention. She had brought them Japanese sweets, spongy gelatinous flower shapes, coated in sugar. She watched as they stuffed their mouths and cheeks. Norah disapproved, and tried to regulate their gobbling. The children threw their arms around Alice's neck, cheeky, mischievous, dragging her again into play, spraying her with sugar.

When the children were in kindergarten, the sisters talked. Norah unfolded the story of her illness. The tests, the results, the eventual surgery. She was philosophical. She had found, she said, a truer self, one tucked inside what she had thought she was. It was a self uncompromising and wide awake. She had started painting again.

'I've returned from somewhere,' she said.

Alice looked at her sister with admiration. Then she told of her life, her travels, her impossible book. Norah was inquisitive about Japan.

'I was there for less than a week; I feel completely ignorant,' Alice confessed. She mentioned Mr Sakamoto, but was secretive about him – not sure what she might say that would preserve him alive and disallow the past tense, or fatalism, or some unthinking wording away of his tenuous presence. Norah sensed his importance.

'Tell me,' she said.

'Later,' Alice replied. 'Later I'll tell you about Mr Sakamoto.'

'Well then, tell me about one special thing that you saw.'

Alice hesitated. She did not want to speak of the museum. Of her fall into the bomb's crater. She sifted images.

'On my last day in Nagasaki, just before I caught the train, in fact, I walked up the steep slope behind my hotel to see the temple of Kannon, the Goddess of Mercy. I had packed in the night and hardly slept; I was just filling in time before I went to the train station. It was first built as a Zen temple, sometime in the seventeenth century, but had of course been destroyed, along with countless artworks inside it, by the atomic bomb. In 1979, the temple was rebuilt, dedicated to the souls of the war dead, and to the victims of the bomb.'

Alice heard her own calm voice, sounding like an historian. Norah nodded.

'The form is very unusual. There's a massive tortoise, a holy tortoise, about thirty feet high, and you enter the temple by walking under the tortoise's neck. Into its body, as it were. Then above the tortoise, riding on its back, is Kannon, a woman in long flowing robes, very poised, very noble. She has a headdress and a halo of multiple spokes, like a star. She's about eighty feet high.'

'This is the memorial?'

'Yes, essentially. Inside, the remains of many bomb victims rest under an altar. There's a tombstone in the shape of a huge metal helmet, under which lie the belongings of soldiers, collected in the Pacific region. And there's a cracked globe tombstone, covering A-bomb victims. In a separate room, outside, are articles found and collected at various battle-grounds. Some have names on them. Canteens. A pair of glasses. If visitors feel entitled, they may claim an item.'

Alice sees again in her memory these small battered things, abandoned in death. Poignant traces. Remains. The detritus, after all, of unmentionable acts and evil prosecutions.

'When I arrived,' continued Alice, 'it was quite early in the morning. I was the only visitor. I wandered around alone, my footsteps echoing, not really sure what I was looking at. A terribly scarred woman, who must have been about ninety years old, appeared from nowhere to act as a guide. She spoke almost no English, but had a handful of nouns, which she simply listed. In any case, I felt I could understand her. She was very humped and bent, about half my height, but she had a great forcefulness to her, a kind of moral insistence. She would say: "Helmet, tomb, Pacific, dead." It was very affect-ing, this loss of conjunctions, this reduction of language. Skeletal translation, I guess. Making do . . .'

Alice paused. The woman had taken her hand. It was a kind of body-memory, now, the warm, dry sensation of fingers between hers, the clasp of a survivor. *Hibakushai.*

'Two other things,' Alice said. 'The old woman took me outside, unlocked a gate, and then a door, and led me under-ground, down high steps, right under the temple. Suspended inside the statue of Kannon is a Foucault's pendulum.'

'What's that?'

'It's a pendulum that demonstrates the rotation of the earth. A perpetual motion device. A heavy ball, swaying at the end of a long rope. The idea, I think, is that it represents prayers for perpetual peace, just as the earth perpetually moves.'

'Ah,' said Norah.

'Perhaps every visitor is shown the pendulum. Perhaps there are real guided tours, with large groups of people and some-one giving details and speaking with authority. But I felt pleased to be taken alone underground, to hold hands with this old woman, to hear her spare list of nouns.'

'The other thing?'

'The other thing is a bell. It tolls every day at 11.02 a.m., the time of the detonation. I was on the train by then. But I was still thinking about the temple. I followed the minute hand on my watch, and at 11.02, on the train, I tried to imagine the bell sounding . . .'

*

Alice wandered around her apartment, unloosened from things. The clock-face kept staring at her. She tried to revise the manuscript of her book on poetics and modernity, but everywhere, on every page, she met Mr Sakamoto. There are texts, she thought, even one's own, full of surprising and unexpected personifications. Texts that summon known faces to fit unknown stories. Novels that split open to reveal one's family. Tales that appear exotic, but drive one home. Recognitions. Returns. Ineluctable associations. Finally she gave up.

She decided to watch old movies on video. From the store Alice brought home Kurosawa's *Ran* and Wellman's *Beau Geste.* *Ran* she put to one side, for another time. She brewed coffee, made toast, and settled to watch *Beau Geste,* and entered with an atavistic sense of relief the black-and-white realm of the three brothers, kitted out gloriously for desert treks and struggles, all good-looking, staunch, bent on heroic sandy death. The Viking funeral scene was very short, and included a pretty young girl as a witness. Mr Sakamoto had never mentioned the presence of the girl. Alice watched until the end. It was maudlin, silly and harsh with racism. Yet she felt brimful of feelings that must have been real: feelings of huge, baffled grief and eroded meaning.

*

The phone rang in the night. Haruko.

'He's gone,' she said simply.

There was a long silence.

'Akiko was with him, at the bedside, but Uncle Tadeo and I were at home, having our dinner.'

Another silence.

'I'm sorry,' said Alice. 'I'm thinking of you all.'

Alice opened a bottle of cabernet sauvignon and toasted Mr Sakamoto. She drank in large gulps from a fashionably over-sized glass. She did not cry. She stared at the night through the window of her apartment. It looked empty, starless.

When at last she slept she dreamed that Mr Sakamoto was a *kamishibai* man. In a library somewhere he opened a small stage with drawstring curtains, clapped the *hyoshigi*, and showed pictures of his life. He had three daughters, Akiko, Haruko and the Bamboo Princess. They all looked alike, and had long black hair trailing down their backs. Uncle Tadeo was there, sitting in the audience with Alice. There was no sound at all. Mr Sakamoto had no voice. Just a sequence of images, almost like silent movies, almost like fairy tales, in which characters appear in emanations of smoky sheen, and then, like moon dwellers, suddenly disappear.

15

The river was a field of light. It might have grown there. Wind
pushed at the brassy water making furrows, rills. A kind of
sigh uprose. Great and lovely possibilities seemed inherent
here, and people on the shore, children especially, sensed
enticing otherworldliness and festive propositions. Strange,
thought Alice, how nature succumbs to abstraction. She
looked from the bank to the far distance and saw ferries, sail
boats, jet-skis, windsurfers, and beyond them, a ridge of
cumulus, efflorescing. To watch this river was to enter into
the openness of things, the space of giving in to lucid and
elemental sensations.

Alice hauled her board and sail onto the water. There was
always the initial shock of cold water to the skin and the slow
saturation. She moved out unsteadily, discerning the depth and
current, and then the wind took her. With a gust like the intake
of a breath, she was swept up, fastened invisibly and carried
away. Alice sped across the water. She felt spray streak up at
her and the tremble of the river beneath. She felt the heave and
slap of the sail and the weight pulling on her shoulders and the
strain at her hips. She adjusted her feet slightly and leaned back
into a cushion of air. Tilted in pure space, finding fleet passage.

What she was seeking, almost without acknowledging it,
was blankness, death. She wanted to fly off into sky and

altogether fade there. Her body felt more than usually heavy, and the wind had a fierceness that made her feel embattled. Better close to the shore, perhaps, where there was more shelter. Alice shifted her position and moved into a jibe, but missed her sail as it swung around, and lost her balance. She plunged into the river. Gasped, swallowed water. Felt the gravity of the river and its implicating enfolding. When her face emerged she was in a mild state of shock. There was a moment like that in Nagasaki, when time dropped away, and she had moved without knowing it. She could see a yacht heading her way and a small motor boat to the left. Keels and propellers were tearing the water. There were serrations, dangers. With great effort she righted her vessel and turned the board, and then, almost instinctually, headed back to dry land. She had seen it, known it: the invitation, out there, to stay under the water. The invitation to sink.

When she reached the shore, Alice discovered a small gash on her thigh. She must have struck something, without realising her injury, a wooden stick, a floating can. Blood joined river water in an impressive pink flow down her leg. Tomorrow, she would accidentally cut her hand. Her body was opening. She was losing integrity.

*

Alice's books embraced her. Sitting at the nexus of book-shelves on three of four walls, she was aware of ordered meanings, clasped together, as if between hands. The promise of things known and described, encased there, sedate, awaiting reception in a single brain. Ghost voices of dead poets, sensible and crazy philosophies, 'humanities' texts each bespeaking an interpreted world. These books expressed Alice's longing for self-completion. She felt their companionship and their economy of subtle satisfactions.

She thought now that they carried, in addition, a kind of privatised mortality.

At her desk, in a shaft of lemon light, Alice was trying to compose a letter to Uncle Tadeo. Almost a week had passed since Haruko's phone call and Alice cast about for words that would in some way honour the immensity of his grief. She failed again and again. What she wrote sounded trite or insincere. She sat at her desk surrounded by trailing sentences and crumpled paper, wishing she could speak to him directly, say something eloquent in Japanese, recite a *haiku*, just a few non-English words. As she was beginning yet another attempt at a letter, Norah's face appeared at her window. She leaned forward, almost pressing her nose to the glass, and tapped with her fingers. Alice opened the front door.

'You've forgotten, haven't you? The tests. They're today.'

She had forgotten. Norah had arranged for Alice to be tested for genetic susceptibility to breast cancer. It was time to hear the results. Norah had been much more concerned than Alice, who was caught up in the swollen world of Mr Sakamoto's passing, and feeling, if anything, neglectful of her own health. Fatalism may have been invading her. Tedious submission. Grief takes away one's own body, deposits it out of reckoning.

They drove together, in Norah's car, to the clinic of genetic research. It was a building beside the hospital in which Margaret was a patient, and it occurred to Alice that they should take the opportunity to visit.

'Not today,' said Norah. 'One thing at a time.'

Her voice was shaky. Her manner was oblique. Alice realised at once that Norah was afraid for her, and that she imagined the worst. She reached to touch her sister's arm on the steering wheel, and Norah flinched with a start, as if she had been recalled from a distant place.

The same grey corridors. The same monstrous lights. Let me never be stuck in hospital, Alice prayed to the ceiling. She began for the first time to feel a little nervous. Odours assailed her, hospital-world entrapments. The specialist looked, disconcertingly, like a doctor on television. He had a square authoritative jaw and an air of calm control. He appeared very young, younger than both of them. His coat was synthetically bright and starched into a crisp neat carapace.

'What's this, then?' he said, pointing to Alice's bandaged hand.

'An accident, that's all. A stupid accident.'

He's stalling, thought Alice. This is the evasion of bad news. In the pause that followed she heard the electric hum of unseen machines. The doctor straightened in his chair.

'I have to tell you,' he said sternly, 'that you are not genetically related. Not at all. You are not of the same family. I assume this fact was unknown to both of you.'

Alice looked at Norah, and saw her release a sob. Whether from relief or surprise, it was difficult to tell.

'There must be a mistake,' Alice said calmly.

'No mistake,' the doctor answered. 'Alice Black, yes? You are in no way related to Norah Black. Nor to Pat Black, who was tested earlier. Norah is the biological daughter of Pat Black; you are not. You're in the clear, by the way.'

Alice rose quickly, upsetting her chair, which fell behind her onto grey carpet with a heavy thud. She was flustered uprighting it and felt the young doctor watching her. She wanted to be away. Away from hospitals. Away from this smug, unconcerned man, who enlaced his hands and seemed, inappropriately, about to crack his knuckles.

'I'm sorry we've wasted your time,' Alice said. She placed her arm around Norah's quaking shoulder and led her from the room. The appointment had lasted less than two minutes.

Alice drove home. Norah wiped her tears and sat quietly, looking straight ahead.

'We're still sisters,' Norah said.

'Of course we are,' Alice responded. But she felt a windy space begin to open inside her, another blasted hollow, another inestimable loss. *Snatched by wind.* Alice drove with grim determination and utmost care. She leaned forward, clutching at the steering wheel like a child at an iron railing. Her bandaged hand made it difficult to steer. When they arrived at the apartment, Norah slid into the driver's seat.

'I have to pick up the kids,' she said. 'But we'll talk later. Promise.'

Norah looked terrible. Strain had reversed her condition, dragged her backwards to the land of the ill. Her eyes were red-rimmed and her hands unsteady on the wheel.

'Later,' she repeated.

*

After all the tries and failures, the message was plain.

Dear Uncle Tadeo,

Hiroshi loved you like a son, and I know you loved him like a father. I am thinking of you daily in this time of deep loss.

Alice.

She sat back in her chair. Uncle Tadeo would understand the brevity, the suspicion of words. Alice remembered his touch on her hair the first time she met him. How uncomplicated it was, how unbroken. She attached to the note a copy of a photograph she had taken of Mr Sakamoto, standing outside their favourite bistro. His tie was a little askew. His expression was relaxed. He held his hands in his pockets and faced the camera with an easy, equitable gaze. He did not look at all like a man who had a few months to live. He looked solid, enduring and charmed by life. A quality of mirth played at the corners of his mouth.

*

She lay in the empty dark, listening to the wind lift the curtains. She had left all the windows open, to attract currents of cooling breeze. There was a gentle hum of traffic and reticulated sprinkler systems. Somewhere, up the road, a party was going on, late into the night. Muffled tones of flirtation, horseplay, mockery, laughter, travelled in an erratic, discontinuous stream, the sounds of other people's lives, other companionships, arousals, conversations. In the mixed-up turmoil of grief and revelation, Alice seemed now to have stopped sleeping altogether. Night-life welcomed her, the rise of the moon, the shift of the stars, the voice of the wind that carried with it − pure vehicle − so many other voices.

When in the morning Alice confronted her parents, it did not go well. She felt as if she had assaulted them.

Fred sat on the velveteen couch, his hands on his knees. He was trying to give up smoking and was agitated and distracted. Pat was in the kitchen, making a pot of tea. Alice heard the water boiling, the setting of tea cups on a tray, the pouring of water into the teapot. When Pat entered she looked pleasantly expectant.

'So, what's the news, then? What's the big secret?'

She put down the tray and began pouring black tea. There was a plate of oatmeal biscuits, a bowl of sugar and a milk jug with a frilled lip that Alice had been fond of since her childhood. Three teaspoons, nesting. She noticed these things vividly, with the force of hallucination. Objects were reclaiming her, wreathing associations, summoning histories. Objects were dividing her by their capture and their wistful implications.

'Why didn't you tell me that I was adopted?'

Pat looked up. Her face stiffened and blanched. Fred said, 'I think I need a ciggie for this,' and rose and left the room to find his tobacco and cigarette papers. Alice and Pat were obliged to wait in shared silence until he returned. Pat gave precise attention to the cups of tea, and shifted the biscuits clockwise, adjusting their circular pattern.

'Christ, you could've warned us,' said Fred, re-entering the room.

'I only just discovered.'

'Even so.'

Fred opened his tobacco pouch on his lap and extracted a few brown threads. Pat and Alice watched in silence as he rolled a cigarette with his thumb and index finger, licked the paper and patted each end on the back of his liver-spotted hand.

'Go on.'

'That's all. I just want to know why I wasn't told.'

Pat was blowing on her tea.

'Fred and I tried for so long,' she said. 'After ten years we still wanted a child, so we decided to adopt. I picked you out,' said Pat quietly, 'because you were crying. The agency took us to see four babies, all lined up, in cots tied with ribbons. We had planned to get a boy, but there you were. Crying your heart out. When I picked you up from the cot you almost immediately settled and I felt so proud of myself, so like a mother. That was that. Then, a few months later, I fell pregnant with Norah, and Fred and I assumed that the pregnancy would go the way of all the others. But then Norah came, so we had two daughters . . .'

'Why didn't you tell me?' Alice insisted. She could hear herself sounding plaintive, like a querulous child.

'We planned to,' said Fred. 'But the time never seemed right. Because you and Norah didn't get along, we both knew it would make things much harder. And then, when you became close, we thought we'd wreck the peace if we told you. And it didn't seem to matter so much. When you loved each other.'

'We always loved each other.'

'Funny ways of showing it.'

Fred was puffing at his cigarette. Pat didn't usually allow smoking in the house, but seemed prepared, on this occasion, to overlook it.

'Maybe we thought you'd guess,' Pat added. 'And ask us.'

'I didn't.'

'No.'

Alice could see that her parents were somehow hurt. Fred was looking away; plucking a fragment of tobacco from his tongue. Pat was blowing on her tea again, her eyes downcast. Alice tried to set things right.

'It doesn't change my love for you both,' she said, sounding unconvincing.

'But we should've told you,' Fred conceded. 'You were bound to find out, sooner or later.'

Estrangement settled upon them. They drank tea in a taut and unfamiliar distance, so that Alice felt she had been crass with the directness of her question. She wanted to know the name of the adoption agency, but couldn't ask now, not yet, anyway. She wanted to say: 'And what do you know of the birth mother? What was she like? What was her name? What name did she give me?'

In a way she did not quite understand, Alice resented this soap-operatic turn in her life, as though her growing up had been a delusion, or a lie, as though this new orphaned self had arrived to make her feel less sure, less authentic, somehow, an impostor daughter.

The room that contained them bore traces of all their lives. Alice raised her teacup and looked ahead. On the mantel-piece were portrait photographs and images of special moments. Pat and Fred's wedding, Alice pushing Norah on a swing, Norah dressed for a formal dance, Alice receiving an award at school, her right hand clasping a rolled certifi-cate. Here were habits and stories, the referential system of personal signs, the shadows of times past. Certain objects replenished memory or pushed it into beige dusty corners. Ornaments of particular ugliness held sweet associations. The immediacy of these things, these family things, these ordinary things knotted into the crisscross of four disparate souls, seized Alice with a force she was not prepared for. A web of connective tissue somehow linked what she saw. She looked across at Pat, caught her quick gaze, and found herself smiling.

*

Alice decided to ring Haruko. It was night time – 8 p.m. – an hour behind the time in Japan. The phone rang and rang, four times, six times, then an answering machine switched itself on. The voice was Mr Sakamoto's. He said something brief in Japanese, and the instructive beep sounded. Alice put down the receiver. Almost immediately she wanted to hear his voice again. Alice dialled the number once more and listened to the same message. Mr Sakamoto's voice fell towards her, recalled his presence, disturbed her with its deep and intrinsic familiarity. The beep sounded, and again Alice replaced the receiver. Then she dialled a third time, not really knowing what she was doing, but strung out, now, wishing to follow the thin thread of his remnant presence, his faint verbal ghost. So much inhered in the brief, untranslated words. In the voice beyond extinction, in this nocturnal recursion. A telephone in Japan. The handset still in its cradle. On the third beep, Alice began to talk.

'Ah, Mr Sakamoto, I have so much to tell you, so much to say. The night is abysmally dark and seems endless without you. What love was it we shared, that played itself out in conversations? What did we know of each other? What understandings? I visited Nagasaki, but was not able to see you. In the museum I thought I saw a glimpse of your childhood; I thought I saw a boy in silhouette, his feet flying up behind him, running down the hill near his home into the site of catastrophe. You were fast and determined. You flew like the wind. I don't know what you saw, but I felt some sympathetic vibration, like the pianos you told me about, a vibration that I took to be the sound we had established between us . . .

'And later, back in Australia, I found again that tonal register with my sister and my family and thought again of Bell, and of your work, and of your long and sweet dedication . . . How you described things. Your stories. Your collection of inventors . . .

'It's lonely without you. I feel I'm floating in space. There is suffocation here. And a dark visor across my eyes. Your carved Spanish astronaut has nothing on me; he's too solid, too visible. I seem to have lost my bearings, with grief for your passing. I seem to have lost certain knowledge of my precious family. They are kind and patient; they know something is wrong; something inside me is missing. To be lost is to be invisible, to have no voice. Uncle Tadeo touched my hair and seemed to understand. Haruko was there, and Akiko, already mourning. I sense how they miss you and join them in sorrow. We are blasted by your leaving. Blown open. Apart. We are full of unspoken words, we, your family. Noise seems everywhere to occur, but none of it is your voice. Rest well, Mr Sakamoto, dear Mr Sakamoto. Rest preserved in that telephone, preserved a little longer, stretching syllables, sentences, across the planet, greeting me in Japanese, in your sure, gentle tone . . .'

*

Alice and Norah were lying with their heads beneath a fig tree. Their legs stretched out into the sunshine. The large leaves shifted sideways in the slight breeze, altering the shade, opening up jagged spaces of light, opening, closing. The sisters had feasted on figs and now were lying on their backs, talking.

'Tell me about Mr Sakamoto,' Norah said.

And in the quietest of voices, Alice began.

Acknowledgements

I am indebted to the Literature Board of the Australia Council for the Arts for the opportunity to work at the Tyrone Guthrie Centre in Ireland, and to the Cité Internationale des Arts for a residence in one of their studios in Paris. These opportunities to work abroad were of inestimable value. I am particularly grateful to Christopher MacLehose of Harvill Secker for his diplomatic encouragement and his suave affirmations. Becky Toyne, Zoë Waldie and Jane Palfreyman have all offered significant support, as have my close friends, to whom I owe more than I can here say. Susan Midalia read my first draft, once again, with enormous generosity and intelligence. My mother, and her Japanese affections, was the consistent inspiration for this novel.